A Candlelight Ecstasy Romance™

"I'VE BEEN WONDERING WHAT IT WOULD BE LIKE TO KISS A BLACKMAILER."

Kane's hands spread across her back and propelled her closer. The apricot silk was no defense against the heat of his palms. Fire licked along her nerve endings as though he were caressing her naked skin.

"You're just not built the way a blackmailer should be built, honey," he growled, burying his lips in the curve of her throat. "You're too soft, too warm, too inviting."

"Please, Kane," Talia heard herself say as she trembled. "Don't call me that!"

"You don't like the sound of blackmail?" he taunted softly. "But it's so effective, darling. Didn't it get you exactly what you wanted?"

CANDLELIGHT ECSTASY ROMANCES™

POWER PLAY

Jayne Castle

A CANDLELIGHT ECSTASY ROMANCE™

Published by
Dell Publishing Co., Inc.
1 Dag Hammarskjold Plaza
New York, New York 10017

Dell ® TM 681510, Dell Publishing Co., Inc.

Candlelight Ecstasy Romance™ is a trademark of
Dell Publishing Co., Inc., New York, New York.

ISBN: 0-440-17067-2

Printed in the United States of America

First printing—September 1982

To Our Readers:

We have been delighted with your enthusiastic response to Candlelight Ecstasy Romances™ and we thank you for the interest you have shown in this exciting series.

In the upcoming months, we will continue to present the distinctive, sensuous love stories you have come to expect only from Ecstasy. We look forward to bringing you many more books from your favorite authors and also, the very finest work from new authors of contemporary romantic fiction.

As always, we are striving to present the unique, absorbing love stories that you enjoy most—books that are more than ordinary romance.

Your suggestions and comments are always welcome. Please write to us at the address below.

Sincerely,

The Editors
Candlelight Romances
1 Dag Hammarskjold Plaza
New York, N.Y. 10017

POWER PLAY

CHAPTER ONE

Talia Haywood responded with conventional politeness to the welcoming smile from Kane Sebastian as she was ushered into his wood-paneled office. But it didn't fool her for a moment. She had learned long ago that smiles and sincere words meant less than nothing from men like this. It was the cool speculation in the startling green eyes that told her what she needed to know.

"Thank you for taking the time to see me, Mr. Sebastian," Talia began formally, accepting a plushly upholstered chair. Outside the tinted glass window of the highrise office building a blistering September sun beat down on the city of Sacramento. But inside the offices of Energy Interface Systems, Inc., all was serenely cool. Including Talia Haywood. She had planned every move of this business call with great care.

"I'm happy to see you, Miss Haywood, but I'm not sure I'm going to be able to be of much help. Our Personnel

Department has already given you the only possible answer."

Talia's smile widened, but there was no warmth in it and her amber eyes flickered briefly with gold as she assessed the man sitting behind the wide mahogany desk.

"You don't have to pretend, Mr. Sebastian. I'm well aware that you're only seeing me because I made such a pest of myself for the past month. Your poor secretary finally made this appointment because I wouldn't give her any peace!"

One heavy chestnut-colored brow rose in reaction to her bluntness and he didn't bother to deny the truth of her words. "Now that you're here," he responded smoothly, "perhaps you'll tell me exactly what it is you want to know."

Talia nodded once, a little abruptly, and prepared to make her request. It wasn't going to be easy getting this man to part with the information she wanted. She had been assessing him since she walked in the door and she knew from the difficulty she'd experienced getting this appointment that he wasn't going to be cooperative. She drew a deep breath and told herself she was as battle-ready as she could be under the circumstances. She had equipped herself with as much ammunition as possible before stepping back into this jungle of a business world which had defeated her so soundly three years earlier.

Her opponent today was, she decided, a typical example of the successful business warrior. In some ways he was probably more ruthless than many because he had started out lacking the expensive university business school education most of his sort had. The sort *she'd* had.

Talia didn't know a great deal about Kane Sebastian, but what little she had managed to find out while preparing for this interview spoke volumes as far as she was concerned.

He had come from nowhere seven years ago to launch Energy Interface Systems, Inc., a thriving company which supplied the drilling and mining products necessary to the large corporations that searched for oil, gas, and coal around the world.

What gossip existed about the man's employment previous to the founding of his company suggested he had spent time working in some of the far-flung oil fields scattered around the globe. Talia couldn't even find documentation to support that simple fact, however.

Whatever his background, there was no denying his current success. It showed in the lean line of a lightweight, Italian-cut summer suit that fit smoothly across broad shoulders and a flat waistline and tapered perfectly to narrow hips and strong thighs. He had risen briefly as Talia was shown into the room and during that short span of time she had found herself overly conscious of the hardness that radiated from the man's body. It wasn't the unyielding strength of his physique that should be worrying her, she thought grimly, but the unyielding combativeness of a mind accustomed to winning the daily battles of the business world.

In the cool light of an overhead fluorescent fixture the deep, chestnut-red of Kane Sebastian's hair gleamed richly. There was enough gray at the temples of the thick pelt which curled softly just above his collar and enough experience in the harshly defined features to make Talia think he was somewhere in his late thirties. Thirty-seven? Thirty-eight?

He was far from being a handsome man, but looks weren't as much a factor for a man in this world as was

13

the ability to project a sense of personal power. Sebastian had that quality to spare. An aggressive nose and an equally forceful chin highlighted a rather hard face. Lines of experience bracketed the firmness of his mouth and marked the corners of the emerald eyes. *A warlock's eyes,* Talia thought irrelevantly. She guessed he stood about six feet tall. Viewed from her own perspective of five-foot-four, that was a little too tall.

It was the eyes that first caught one's attention, though, Talia decided dispassionately. They were cold green gems set above high, deeply tanned cheekbones. And they were definitely not smiling in a polite echo of the mouth. Instead there was deep speculation in the green depths. *As well there might be,* Talia thought bracingly. After all, he knew she wanted something from him.

And what, she wondered with silent sarcasm, did he think she was prepared to do in order to achieve her goal? If he thought of trying the old game of encouraging her to prostitute herself in exchange for the information she wanted, he had a surprise coming.

Or would he even be superficially interested in her enough to use that tactic? Somehow Talia doubted that she was Kane Sebastian's type. A man like this would prefer ornamental, blue-eyed blondes who cuddled and cooed for their supper and diamond bracelets.

Talia wasn't blond. The wealth of hair which was twisted into a sleek, severe knot at the back of her head was a deep, tawny brown in color. The large, slanting, amber eyes mirrored an intelligence which would have stood her in better stead if it hadn't been for the underlying vulnerability.

Talia also didn't consider herself particularly ornamental. She knew the straight nose, high forehead, and full mouth comprised a reasonably attractive face, but she was aware the combination lacked glamor. In its place was a certain suspicion of softness. That softness, unfortunately, reflected an internal characteristic which Talia despised in herself. It made her vulnerable, unable to fight the savagely civilized battles of the corporate world.

The softness she sensed in herself was also there in her slender five-foot-four-inch frame. High, full breasts and gently flaring hips lacked the willowy lines that would have given her a more sophisticated look and a female equivalent of the internal power radiating from Kane Sebastian. She was thirty years old and she would have liked some of that power.

At least her wheat-colored suit, with its fitted jacket and pleated skirt, was a match for the expensive outfit Sebastian wore, she decided in some humor. And the azure silk blouse underneath lent a degree of coolness to her businesslike attire.

"Did your Personnel Manager inform you just what I'm seeking, Mr. Sebastian?" She plunged in determinedly.

"You've requested details on a former employee of ours, I believe," Kane murmured a little cautiously. "You must know it is definitely not standard practice to release that sort of information to anyone. What with all the new legislation protecting privacy—"

"I'm willing to settle for your Personnel Department contacting this individual and relaying the message that I'm trying to get in touch with him," Talia interrupted, having heard all the excuses from the Personnel Manager. "Surely that's not a violation of your, er, company ethics?"

"Am I to assume from the tone of voice behind that last comment that you don't think my company has much in the way of ethics?" Once again the red brow lifted, this time quellingly. The quirking smile that tilted the corner of his mouth was not quite indulgent.

Talia parted her lips to tell Kane exactly what she thought of modern corporate ethics and then bit her tongue. There was no need to deliberately antagonize him at this point. She still might be able to get what she wanted by simple logic and persuasion.

"I'm aware that your firm must operate within certain laws," she managed by way of a substitute comment. "And I'm not asking you to violate those laws. If you can't give me Justin Gage Westbrook's current address, you could at least notify him that I'm trying to get in touch."

"You've been very persistent in your inquiries, I under- stand," Kane observed, rising from the leather chair he had been occupying and moving toward one of the tinted windows. He appeared to be studying the dome of the state capitol building a few blocks away. "Would you mind telling me why it's so important that you get in touch with this man? You've indicated to Personnel that it is not a life-or-death matter and you have no family connection, according to my manager."

"It's almost a family connection," Talia said quietly, watching the set of Sebastian's head as he surveyed the Sacramento landscape. She tried to judge his mood. Was he making up his mind whether or not to be helpful or was he turning her request over and over mentally, seeking some personal benefit for himself? She had a hunch the latter was the case. It would be instinctive for him. Still, he might decide to cooperate if she made a reasonable case.

"What do you mean by that?" he asked, swinging around abruptly and trapping her critical gaze.

16

"My father and Mr. Westbrook were close friends."

"But it isn't your father making the request."

"My father is dead, Mr. Sebastian," Talia informed him stonily. "He was killed in a car accident five years ago."

"I see. I'm sorry." The short apology was definitely stark. Sebastian continued to eye her with a narrowed, analytical look. A tragedy five years in the past would not warm any sentimental streak that might be in his nature, Talia guessed cynically. "Then perhaps you will explain your persistence in getting in contact with Westbrook? I must warn you that I seriously doubt we can be of any assistance. According to our records he worked for us only briefly a few years ago and in a somewhat limited capacity."

"I'm aware of that limited capacity." Talia half-smiled.

There was a perceptible hesitation in his manner. "You seem to have done a very thorough job of tracking down Justin Westbrook," Kane finally said softly.

Talia shrugged. "It's been a hobby of mine for years."

"Years!" He looked a little dumbfounded.

Talia laughed at his astonished expression. "A hobby, Mr. Sebastian. Some people collect stamps or foreign cars. I collect information on Justin Gage Westbrook." For a moment genuine amusement danced in her amber eyes, lighting tiny flecks of gold. Kane watched her with interest.

"A little unusual . . ." he began thoughtfully.

"It's been a challenge, I'll admit. But over the years I've amassed a wealth of correspondence dealing with Westbrook. It's amazing what sort of information can be obtained from perfectly legitimate sources if one is extremely patient." Talia couldn't keep some of the satisfaction out of her voice. Tracing Justin Gage Westbrook to Sebastian's company was the closest she had ever come to finding the elusive man. She was not about to let the firm's unwillingness to release information on former employees get in her way now.

"May I ask why you've gone to such an effort?"

Talia smiled as he resumed his seat. "As I told your Personnel Manager when he asked, I can't claim it's a life-and-death matter. But there was a long-time friendship between Westbrook and my father and when I was a child he was a frequent visitor to our home. And, occasionally, there were gifts . . ."

"Gifts for you?"

"Yes. Strange little toys from faraway places," Talia murmured, her eyes briefly hinting at the exotic daydreams those toys had touched off in an only child who thrived on mystery and romance.

"So Westbrook was a long-time family friend," Kane summed up briskly, as if deliberately breaking the tenuous touch of intrigue that had entered the atmosphere.

Talia nodded, pleased at his statement. Perhaps he did understand. . . .

"In that case, Miss Haywood, I think Westbrook would have contacted your or your father some time ago. The fact that he hasn't indicates he either does not wish to pursue the friendship or the possibility that he may no longer be alive. He would be in his sixties by now, according to the short file we have on him."

Kane's crisp response told Talia all she needed to know. He was determined to be unhelpful. She sighed inwardly and decided on another approach.

"He may, indeed, no longer be alive. In fact, according to the last official information I have on him, he died somewhere in Africa while employed by an international relief agency. About a year after he worked for you."

"In that case . . ." Kane looked at her questioningly.

"I would like to confirm it. The body was never recovered, you see, and I feel there are some unknown factors. Well, never mind. I just want to confirm his death, if possible."

"For the sake of putting an end to your hobby?" he asked skeptically, leaning forward and resting his elbows on his desk as he studied her intently.

"In a sense . . ."

"I hardly think that's a legitimate reason for Energy Interface Systems to become involved in a personal matter like this." But there was a waiting quality in Kane Sebastian's words, as if he were making the statement merely to draw out her next line of offense.

Something crackled in the air between them for a moment and Talia felt a restlessness pervade her body. A curious alertness seemed to grip her senses. She resisted the urge to get to her feet and pace the room. Very uncool, she told herself wryly.

She knew the source of the unease. There was a tauntingly familiar glitter deep in that emerald gaze that studied her so deliberately—a wholly masculine, wholly primitive gleam that she had seen before in men like this, successful men who got nearly everything they went after and whose superficial emotions enabled them to enjoy only the hunt.

It was an instinct, this ability to analyze a situation, decide how it could best be used for personal advantage, and then go for the jugular. An instinct shared by men and women alike who made it to the top. An instinct Talia

Haywood had discovered that she lacked. Her career had been ruined because of this peculiar, predatory quality.

But she had come too far and this lead on Justin Westbrook was too interesting to ignore. It had taken a great deal to steel herself for the return to Sacramento, the scene of her personal disaster three years ago. She wasn't about to give up just because the man who held this particular key in the puzzle was now surveying her with that appraising, probing glance.

"Are you saying you won't help me, Mr. Sebastian?" She kept her voice cool and icily calm.

"I'm saying we probably can't help you, and even if we could, your reasons so far aren't adequate to justify the use of my employees' time and energy. If you have a more compelling justification, I might be willing to ask my people to send a note of inquiry to the last address we had for Westbrook . . ."

He let the sentence trail off with the implication that he seriously doubted that she could come up with anything more important than sheer female curiosity.

"What, precisely, would constitute more compelling justification?" Talia inquired dryly.

Instead of answering the question, Kane rested his chin thoughtfully on the heel of his palm. There was a long pause.

"Why," he finally asked, "does your name ring a bell? I know we've never met. I'd never forget that haughty little chin or those challenging gold eyes. So why do I keep trying to place you?"

Talia started, an unwelcome warmth creeping up into her cheeks. It wasn't only his personal comment on her features that made her grit her teeth, it was the unpleasant fact that he remembered something from somewhere.

How many other people in the Sacramento business community also remembered? God! She wanted to get her answers and get out of town.

"As you say, we've never met," she retorted repressively. "Perhaps you once knew someone else with a name similar to mine."

"Not likely. I've never known a woman named Talia. It's unusual." He smiled. The expression reminded her vaguely of a wolf.

"Then I'm afraid I can't help your memory," Talia shot back with a cool note of dismissal. "Now, about my request. All I ask is that you either give me Westbrook's last address or have someone send a note to it. I admit the odds are that it will be returned as undeliverable, but I've checked out colder leads and occasionally come up with something."

"What are you hoping to find? If you already have official word of his death, any lead you got from an old address would probably only take you up to the point of his disappearance. Which you already know about. Circular logic, I'm afraid."

"That's my problem, Mr. Sebastian. I've learned that you never know what you'll come up with."

"You've checked out all the angles?" he inquired mildly.

"Every last one I came across. As I said, I've collected quite a pile of correspondence. Each piece adds a little more information."

"I commend your perseverance," Kane applauded dryly. "Now, why does your name haunt me?" he added, proving he could be just as persevering.

"I haven't the faintest idea!" Talia's brows came together over her straight nose. She wanted him off that tack.

The wolfish smile broadened mockingly. "Perhaps we should make a deal."

"A deal?"

"You satisfy my curiosity and I'll think about trying to satisfy yours."

"But that's impossible!" Talia exclaimed, lying through her teeth. "How can I possibly guess why my name sounds familiar to you?"

"Try," he suggested amiably.

"Why are you being so difficult, Mr. Sebastian? I'm here with a very simple request. Surely it can't be too much of an imposition on you to ask one of your clerks in Personnel to dig up Westbrook's old address. You only have to pick up the phone—"

"Let's see," he interrupted, not paying the least attention to her plea. "You look like a woman who has some familiarity with the business world. Proper little suit, pumps, neatly styled hair, and no loud, clashing jewelry. Are you a businesswoman, Miss Haywood?"

"I teach, Mr. Sebastian," she said tightly.

"A teacher?" he affected surprise. "Now that I wouldn't have guessed. What do you teach? Nuclear physics? Mathematics? French literature?"

Talia felt a kind of nervous dread. She didn't like the telltale signs. This whole thing was rapidly becoming a game for him, and games with men like this were played for high stakes. She needed to douse the humor in those emerald eyes.

"I doubt that my work could be of interest to you." Talia kept her voice as matter-of-fact as possible.

"On the contrary. If I knew what you taught, I might be able to figure out the connection."

He waited with an expression of polite hopefulness

22

which didn't fool her for a minute. He wasn't going to let her get back to her own question until she'd satisfied his. Talia knew her only option at that moment was to walk out the door, and she couldn't bear to do that. Not after coming this far.

"I work for an organization that gives seminars and short courses focusing on various problems in business management." Talia sincerely hoped the bitterness didn't show. It wasn't directed at him, it was directed at herself. She was teaching such classes for the simple reason that she hadn't been able to handle the real-life situation.

Kane was grinning. "Is that another way of saying you teach assertiveness training?"

"That certainly comes into the program!"

"I get the feeling you're practicing some of the techniques on me." He chuckled.

"Now that I've answered your question, Mr. Sebastian," Talia began with as much assertiveness as she could muster.

"But you haven't. I still don't know why your name should be familiar. I've certainly never attended one of your seminars!"

"It might not be a bad idea if you did," she gritted, unable to resist. "You might get some helpful guidance out of the one on uses and abuses of executive power!"

"Uses and abuses of . . . wait a minute!" Kane sat back in his chair with a decisive movement and Talia could have groaned aloud. "I've got it now. You're Talia Haywood, aren't you?"

"Of course I'm Talia Haywood," she snapped, angry at having provided the clue he needed. She could almost see the relays closing in his agile mind. "I've told you that already!"

He shook his head impatiently, the red-brown of his hair catching the overhead light in a movement which, for some reason, briefly caught her attention.

"No, no, I mean you're *the* Talia Haywood. The bright up-and-coming young manager over at Darius & Darnell Industries. The one on the fast track to a vice-presidency . . . until you made the mistake of trying to find an even faster track via the bedroom." He was on his feet, a long, gliding stride taking him back to the window where he turned to confront her interestedly. "Or so the papers implied. You were quite a topic of conversation three years ago as I recall."

Talia had whitened under the impact of his words. The skin across her knuckles grew taut as she grasped the arms of her chair and faced him with a fierce pride.

"Now that you've satisfied your nagging curiosity, may we return to the main subject?" she demanded acidly.

"Did you?" he asked simply, ignoring her query.

"Did I what?" Confused for an instant, she glared at him.

"Did you sleep with, what was his name? Hazelett? No, Hazelton. I think that was the name of the president over at Darius & Darnell at the time, wasn't it? And you were his fair-haired girl . . ." The last words were accompanied by a mocking glance at her tawny-brown hair. It was as if they were discussing a delightful tidbit of gossip.

Which, thought Talia savagely, was exactly what she had been three years ago. Gossip fodder.

"It is not a subject I wish to discuss. No one believed me three years ago. There's no reason to think anyone would believe me today. I'm here to talk about Justin Gage Westbrook." It took an unbelievable amount of control to refrain from leaping to her feet and crossing the room to strike his hard, tanned face.

"You're telling me you weren't sleeping with him?"

"I'm not telling you anything about that mess! It's over and done with," she hissed, feeling her control slipping and hating herself for not being able to handle her emotions better. But on this one topic she still felt wounded and horribly vulnerable. "About Justin Westbrook . . ."

Kane sighed as if pulled away from a juicy steak. The green eyes flickered again with the speculation she had seen the moment she'd been ushered into his office. He moved slowly back toward his desk.

"Yes, about Mr. Westbrook," he repeated slowly. "As I've said, I don't see what good it would do you to have us try and contact his old address."

She knew he was going to refuse. Probably the only reason he hadn't refused outright in the beginning was because of his own personal curiosity. Well, she'd satisfied that curiosity, Talia thought, inwardly raging. Damned if he was going to get away with such a one-sided deal!

"I have," she interrupted coldly, "a reason or two you may wish to consider before refusing my request." She steeled herself, already a little appalled at what she planned. But her anger was still riding high and Kane Sebastian was so infuriatingly in charge, or so he thought.

He blinked, the long lashes over the green jewels lowering with a dangerous laziness. He sat propped on the corner of the desk and waited.

Talia drew a deep breath, sensing the new menace in the atmosphere. She didn't want to resort to this. It wasn't her style. She knew that better than anyone else in the world. And if Sebastian hadn't goaded her, she would never had

25

tried it. Grimly she reminded herself she was back in the vicious corporate world. The only language a wolf like this would understand would be the tactics common to that world.

"I am aware, Mr. Sebastian, of what Justin Westbrook does or did for a living and I know you are also aware of his rather unusual career. I seriously doubt you normally put people on your payroll for a few short weeks and then release them."

"All the time, Miss Haywood," he drawled. "All the time. They're called consultants."

Talia nodded, her mouth curving in a satisfied, knowing smile. "Justin has been called a great many things in his time, according to the correspondence and records I've managed to accumulate. You were not the first to put him on the payroll as a consultant. But don't bother telling me you did so of your own accord. You were asked to do so, weren't you, Mr. Sebastian?"

He regarded her from beneath the lazily lowered lids, his smile as cool as her own. "Exactly what have you found out about the mysterious Mr. Westbrook that makes you say that, Miss Haywood?"

"He was a spy during the time he worked for you in South America, Mr. Sebastian," she declared easily, the excitement which had brought her this far flaring to life once more in her amber eyes. "And you knew it. I may not be able to prove it from the information I've got, but I learned a long time ago that one doesn't have to prove something in order to cause a great deal of damage."

"What, exactly, are you trying to say?" Kane ground out very softly.

"I have no quarrel with your decision to assist the United States Government by providing cover for one of its

26

agents," Talia murmured, nerving herself for the next bit, "but there are many who frown on business involving itself with espionage in foreign countries. A little publicity to that effect could seriously damage the image of Energy Interface Systems, Inc., couldn't it?"

The green eyes were quite frozen now. Talia barely repressed a shiver.

"Are you by any chance threatening me with blackmail if I refuse to help you locate Westbrook?" Kane finally asked a little too gently.

Talia's mocha-colored nails dug into the arm of her chair as she refused to be intimidated. She inclined her head in a negligent movement of acquiescence, saying nothing. She had fired her biggest weapon. All she could do now was wait for the effect.

"So." Kane drummed his fingers on the mahogany desk in a seemingly absent manner. "You appear to have come a long way since you left town three years ago, Miss Haywood. As I recall, you didn't put up much of a fight when Hazelton started slinging innuendos around." He paused, but Talia refused to be drawn out.

"But here you are, three years later, fully prepared to resort to blackmail merely to get the answer to a question."

Talia swallowed but kept her gaze level and unflinching.

"You don't appear to give me much choice," Kane observed.

Talia got to her feet, amazed her legs didn't collapse under her.

"Here's the phone number of my hotel. If you come up with anything by this evening, please give me a call." She reached into her chocolate leather shoulder bag and pulled out a card.

27

Placing it neatly in front of him on the polished wooden desk, she turned and walked out the door. If what she was feeling was a foretaste of victory, Talia wasn't sure she was going to like it.

As she walked out to the white Peugeot she'd left standing beside the curb, she was still asking herself where she'd found the nerve to resort to blackmail. What was it about Kane Sebastian that had pushed her that far? Or was she, indeed, a different person from what she had been three years ago?

CHAPTER TWO

Talia was on her fifth lap of the hotel's pool before she finally acknowledged that she was trying to exhaust herself. She shook back her hair, the wet tendrils cascading slickly down between her shoulder blades as she reached the side and paused to draw breath.

It was nearly six o'clock and the crystal water still retained the heat of the day's sun. Talia had the pool to herself. She had heard nothing from Kane Sebastian and at five she'd abandoned her watch on the phone in her room in favor of working out some of her restlessness.

Had he decided to call her bluff? Talia chewed nervously on her lower lip as she clung to the tiled edge of the pool. A bluff was all it had been, of course. She would never go to the newspapers with her information. Her only hope was that Sebastian didn't suspect the full extent of her weakness.

That thought was enough to send her slicing headlong once more through the refreshing water. This time she did the entire lap under the surface, emerging in a splashing rush on the far side.

Eyes still shut tightly against the chlorine-laced water streaming down her face, Talia blindly groped for the side of the pool and heaved herself lightly to a sitting position, legs dangling over the side. She was fumbling for her towel, when it was thrust helpfully into her hand.

"Thanks," she mumbled breathlessly, drying her face quickly and lifting her eyes to the man standing beside her. Even without her contacts she recognized the finely striped Italian suit. "Kane!"

"Think nothing of it," he told her wryly. "We blackmail victims learn to be extremely accommodating."

Talia scrambled hastily to her feet, taken aback to find him beside her. A brusque phone call with the information she wanted was the most she had expected or desired. She had no desire to see her "victim" again in person!

"You . . . you didn't phone," she said hurriedly, wrapping the small white hotel towel around her as best she could. Kane might be a victim, but the raking glance he was giving her body didn't have a particularly humble quality. The strapless cranberry maillot suddenly seemed insufficient cover for her rounded breasts and full hips.

"I thought I ought to talk to you in person, given the circumstances. We can discuss the situation over dinner," Kane said crisply, moving one foot out of the way as she stood, dripping, near it.

"Dinner! I see no reason to have dinner. Just say what you have to say and—"

"It's not that simple," he told her irritably, green eyes narrowing. "And since I spent the past few hours going through the files personally, the least you could do is agree to take me to dinner for my efforts. I'm starved!"

She stared up at his righteously aggrieved expression and relented. It sounded as if he were going to give her what she wanted. She could afford to be polite at this stage.

"All right, Kane . . . Mr. Sebastian. Let me get dressed and I'll be with you shortly."

"Make it Kane. Surely it's proper for a blackmailer and her victim to be on a first-name basis?" he murmured smoothly.

Talia flushed and started quickly toward the pool gate. "I'll meet you in the lounge adjoining the restaurant."

"Fine," he declared, following her through the gate. "I'll be the one waiting in a dark corner with a properly defeated look on my face."

Well, at least he didn't sound terribly angry, Talia thought, feeling vastly relieved as she hastened down the hall to her room. Perhaps he'd decided to be a good sport about the whole thing. The attitude astonished her, but she was too grateful to question her luck. Letting herself inside the room, she made for the shower, mentally going through the small wardrobe she'd brought along.

The low-necked apricot silk with its flouncy hemline looked perfect for a late summer evening, she decided, slipping it on and tying the soft, gold sash. Kane was wearing the suit he'd had on earlier and she could have put hers on again, but something in her wanted to wear the silk tonight. She stepped into high-heeled sandals with gold metallic strips on the heels, fastened a gold chain around her neck, and picked up her small mesh bag.

Stopping to survey her image critically in the mirror before heading out the door, Talia decided the sleek lines of her still-damp hair, which she had twisted into a curve

31

at the nape of her neck, added a sufficient touch of austerity to the total look.

She walked into the lounge feeling a strange sense of anticipation that she insisted to herself must be due to the fact that she had been successful in dealing with Kane Sebastian. She still couldn't believe it! He hadn't been astute enough to call her bluff, so she must have appeared very, very determined. If only she'd had the same amount of courage three years ago . . . Well, it was too late to think about the mistakes of the past.

Talia swept gracefully, even a bit jubilantly, toward the small table in the corner, recognizing the lean, hard frame draped casually in the chair.

Kane got to his feet as she approached, seating her politely.

"A margarita?" he suggested easily. "They make very good ones here. Not the syrupy sweet sort. On a hot day they're exactly what the doctor ordered."

"That will be fine, thank you."

"Don't thank me," he growled. "You're picking up this tab. It's the least you can do."

Talia smiled at him, her sense of humor beginning to resurface. "Some victims don't seem to know their place." When he grinned back, she ignored the slightly wolfish impression. "Now, tell me what you found out," she ordered eagerly.

"In a minute." He signaled a cocktail waitress and gave their order. When he turned back to face Talia, the familiar gleam of speculation and curiosity was back in his eyes. "Don't get too excited. It's not all cut and dried, as I told you out at the swimming pool."

"What's the problem? Either you are going to contact the last address you have or you aren't—"

"The last address," he retorted blandly, "was a tiny little village in South America. What do you think the odds are that he ever returned or that a letter to him would even reach the place?"

Talia's eyes widened with the rush of disappointment she was feeling. "South America! You don't have a stateside address?"

"No."

"Oh," she muttered, "I was so hoping that this time I would get somewhere. I thought I was so close!"

He eyed her as she digested the discouraging news, not saying anything else until the tequila-and-lime drinks had been served.

"You're really into this search, aren't you? You must be if you're willing to resort to threats to get people to help you. How many people have you blackmailed for answers, Talia Haywood?" He sipped at his drink, watching her over the salt-edged rim.

Talia flinched, sitting back in her chair and lifting her own glass. "You were my first such attempt," she forced herself to say flippantly. "I hadn't had the right combination of circumstances to try it before!"

"I'm flattered," he responded dryly. "What led you to me?"

"The cumulative clues in a pile of letters from various government bureaucrats," she admitted. "By contacting one agency after another over the years I've managed to trace Westbrook from Korea to Southeast Asia, the Middle East and finally, South America. I have doubts about Africa."

"And somewhere, some helpful government clerk uncovered the fact that Westbrook had gone to work for my firm?"

33

"In their efforts to give people like Westbrook a realistic cover, the government manages to create a paper trail that can be followed, if one knows what one is looking for." Talia shrugged.

"And you knew the primary fact—that Justin Westbrook was an agent?"

"My father told me years ago. It was no secret in our household, although we knew nothing concrete about Justin's actual work. At least, I didn't. I'm not so sure about my father," Talia added reminiscently. "I have a suspicion they worked together for a while. But after Korea Dad married and started a family. He went into business and built a home. But that life-style wasn't for Justin, I guess. He was a man who thrived on action and excitement."

"What about your mother? Is she still alive?" There was a genuine curiosity in the question.

"Very much so." Talia laughed. "She's taken herself off to see the world. Signed up for a round-the-world cruise. I think she's having a great time, but it's hard to tell. She's too busy to write very often!" Talia's smile subsided as she went on reflectively. "I think she always saw Justin as more of a threat to her marriage than anything else. She told me once how one Christmas he'd swooped down on us out of nowhere, bearing gifts and trying to entice Dad into going back to work with him again. He was on his way to another exotic country and it must have sounded pretty exciting to Dad. I think Mom was really afraid he'd go with Justin. But Dad managed to put responsibility to his new family first, much to my mother's relief. I think Mom was just as happy to have Justin busy far away. We saw him once or twice after that, but then the occasional letters stopped coming and there were no more handmade toys from strange places. Mom and Dad figured Justin had probably gotten himself killed."

"And one day you decided to find out for sure?"

"I read a lot of adventure fiction," Talia apologized ruefully. "It struck me that there was a real-life adventure and mystery waiting to be solved right in my own back-yard. So a few years ago I dug out all the old letters from Justin Westbrook to my parents and started hunting for clues. I found his service record easily enough and from there on I just kept writing and asking questions."

"I think," Kane said surprisingly, "that I can under-stand something of the appeal of your hobby." He chuck-led hoarsely. "I read a lot of adventure stories myself while I was growing up. If I'd had a genuine James Bond in the family, I might have wound up doing the same thing you are. But I have a word of advice for you."

"What's that?" Talia asked warily.

"Be careful who you go around blackmailing. Not ev-eryone gives up and caves in as easily as I did," he told her smoothly. "Some folks might get downright hostile."

Talia heard the warning in his voice, but she chose to ignore it. "I did a good job of selecting my first victim, don't you think? Had my answer within a few hours, even if it wasn't all that helpful," she retorted lightly, not want-ing to admit just how relieved she was that the nasty business was behind her. "To tell you the truth, if you hadn't pushed me so hard about my past, I probably wouldn't have gotten mad enough to resort to blackmail!"

"I'm not so sure about that," Kane said coolly. "I had the feeling you didn't particularly like me the moment you walked through my door. Why was that, Talia? I had the feeling I'd been tried and convicted before I even had a chance to find out what the charges were." He looked at

35

her almost whimsically. "What *were* the charges, Miss Haywood?"

"You're imagining things, Kane," she told him firmly. "I was a little tense because I thought I was so close to getting some answers about Justin Westbrook. That's all. Speaking of those answers, I expect you to at least try a letter to that little Latin American town. Perhaps someone there will remember him. Better yet, why don't you give me the name of the place and I'll do it?"

"I'll have a letter of inquiry sent, Talia, don't worry. I know when I'm beaten. Now do you mind taking me in to dinner? I'm still hungry."

He got to his feet, but not before Talia had caught the irritated glitter in his eyes. Kane Sebastian wasn't very pleased over having let himself be persuaded into parting with the minimal information in his files.

"She'll take care of it," he told the cocktail waitress who hurried toward them with the check. He indicated Talia with a casual thumb.

"I'll have to take care not to be swept off my feet by your gallantry," Talia grumbled, pulling out a charge card.

"The price of doing business," he returned, taking her arm as she finished signing the slip.

The price of doing business with Kane Sebastian rose steadily after that. Talia endured patiently as he ordered a horrendously expensive Napa Valley Cabernet, clams Bordelaise as hors d'oeuvre, and chateaubriand with a Caesar salad.

"For the price of your dinner I could probably buy that entire South American village," Talia remarked, glancing down at her own modest poached salmon.

He grinned cheerfully, cutting his rich meat with gusto.

36

"I'm trying to teach you to think twice before you stoop to blackmail again."

"If I'd known how little help you were going to be, I might have avoided it the first time!"

But his teasing, expensive as it was proving to be, seemed to set the tone for the evening. In effect a truce had been called. Kane had submitted to her demands with reasonably good grace and Talia reminded herself that clues had turned up in more unlikely situations. Something might turn up in that forgotten little village. And if it didn't, she would shrug and accept the outcome philosophically. She'd followed a lot of dead-end leads before.

By the time Kane was choosing between the two most expensive items on the dessert menu, Talia realized a new element had crept into the atmosphere between them. Perhaps it was because she'd won her small victory and intimidated him into not calling her bluff. Perhaps it was because Kane had avoided the subject of her career disaster. Or perhaps it was simply because Kane Sebastian could be very charming over a dinner table. Whatever the reason, Talia was feeling comfortably in charge of the situation by the time the dinner check was handed over to her with a flourish.

She identified the basis of the feeling as she carelessly signed her name to the large bill for dinner. She was no longer afraid of him.

No longer afraid? Yes, she thought grimly. She'd been very much afraid of the man when she'd walked into his office. Afraid of all he represented. Afraid she could not hold her own against a man who had succeeded brilliantly where she had failed three years earlier. Afraid of reentering the world she'd fled in disgrace.

No, she was no longer afraid of him. She'd managed to

make a very shrewd, very tough businessman give her what she wanted. Dinner suddenly seemed very cheap indeed. She was more than happy to humor him now.

"Care to share the joke?" he broke into her thoughts to ask as she put the charge card back into her mesh bag.

"A private one, I'm afraid," Talia demurred, rising gracefully.

"Ah, yes. A private joke. I understand. I hope you're enjoying it." He took her arm once again and guided her out of the elegant dining room. "How long will you be staying in Sacramento?"

"I was planning on driving back to San Jose in the morning."

"Not going to wait around for the response to my inquiry?" he asked as they strolled across the shadowy patio toward the entrance to Talia's wing of the hotel.

"It will probably be a long time coming, if ever." Talia sighed, lifting her face to the balmy breeze. "I'll trust you to get in touch when you hear something."

"I might hear something within a couple of days," he said silkily.

"What? But a letter will take forever to get there!" She stopped, turning on her heel to confront him.

"I sent a cable this afternoon," he told her, smiling. "With any luck I might get a response tomorrow. If there's any response to be had, that is. If not tomorrow then perhaps in a day or two."

Her eyes sparkled with sudden excitement as she looked up at him in the soft moonlight. "In that case I think I'll stick around a day or two," she announced, coming to an immediate decision. "I'll phone my boss and get someone else to cover my classes."

Kane nodded blandly, resuming the strolling pace and

tugging her along beside him. "I'll contact you in the morning then."

"Or as soon as you hear anything, anything at all!"

"Yes, ma'am," he agreed obediently.

"Oh, Kane!" Talia breathed impulsively, halting once more as they reached her door. "Thank you. Thank you very much."

He said nothing, one chestnut brow rising in self-mockery as he inserted her key into the lock.

"I know I forced you into this," Talia said quickly, reaching out to touch his sleeve in an unconscious gesture of supplication and apology. "But I really am grateful for any help you can give me. You don't know how much this means to me!"

He stared down at her enigmatically for a moment, the door open, the key dangling in his hand as they entered the hotel room. As Talia met his eyes she was abruptly aware of the heat and power in him, standing so close. And she'd held her own with him!

The green eyes narrowed slightly but not with anger. Her feminine instincts identified the simmering glow and responded. He wanted to kiss her, Talia realized with a tingling sensation.

What did she want? An uncertainty she would never have expected to feel around a man like this was overwhelming her. This morning the idea would have been unthinkable. She disliked men like this intensely. Since the disaster three years ago she'd been careful to stay clear of men who viewed the world from a predator's point of view.

But she was in control of this situation, Talia reminded herself. She'd held her own against Kane Sebastian. And, in spite of its beginnings, the evening had turned out to be an enjoyable one. What harm could there be in a kiss?

The strangely jubilant sensation which had nibbled at her all evening and which she attributed to her success in chasing down one more clue to Justin Gage Westbrook surged through her again, bathing Talia in an exciting warmth. Her amber eyes were golden now, but not with anger.

"Thank you for the dinner and drinks, Talia," Kane whispered a little huskily, a small, anticipatory smile playing at the edge of his mouth. "You know, after a meal like that, I'm willing to let a woman kiss me on the first date."

Talia caught her breath, aware of a dampness on her palms. How ridiculous! All he was suggesting was a goodnight kiss. And after the threats she'd made this afternoon, it was rather generous of him not to hold any grudge.

Slowly, feeling almost hypnotized by his proximity, Talia lifted her fingertips to touch the side of his cheek. Standing on tiptoe in the delicate sandals, she brushed her mouth lightly against his in a butterfly's caress.

All her senses seemed to open to him in that brief moment. She knew the feel of his skin under her fingertips, the scent of his body coming at her in a warm wave of musky heat mixed with the remnants of his aftershave and the cool firmness of his mouth beneath hers.

It was too much, and belatedly Talia realized it. She had no business being this affected, this intrigued, this entranced by a virtual stranger. What was the matter with her?

But even as she summoned the willpower to step back, the opportunity to retreat was lost.

Kane's arms closed around her as if she had walked into

40

the trap she'd sensed earlier in the day. She was caught in a heated grip of steel and velvet. His kiss seemed to explode about her in a soft haze as he took control of the embrace.

"Kane, I . . ."

"I've been wondering since this morning what it would be like to kiss a blackmailer," he said huskily against her lips before claiming them in a sensuous, disturbing movement that parted them beneath his onslaught.

Talia's gasp was muffled as his tongue slipped erotically along the barrier of her teeth—teasing, probing, persuading.

Kane groaned and his body shifted to receive hers as his hands spread across her back and propelled her closer. The apricot silk was no defense against the heat of his palms. Fire licked along her nerve endings as though he were caressing her naked skin.

Talia knew she was responding. She had been responding to this man on a bewildering variety of levels all day. She had disliked him, feared him, conquered him, held her own with him, and been charmed by him even as she picked up the tab for his dinner. For her body, this was merely the next logical step.

She moaned as his hands slid farther down the silk to her waist and sought the base of her spine.

When he found the sensitive area and began a gentle kneading, Talia's response rose still higher. She allowed him into the honeyed secret of her mouth, thrilling unbelievably to the small invasion.

He tasted her intimately, his body hardening against hers. Unable to resist the impulse, Talia snagged his questing tongue with her own, offering a daring duel which was at once accepted.

As she fought the sensuous battle, striving to break into the secret arena of his mouth, Talia felt Kane shape the curve of her buttocks, drawing her deeply into the cradle of his taut thighs. Then one hand began sliding upward.

Slowly, invitingly, the caressing fingers roamed higher, gliding along her ribcage until they barely touched the underside of her breast.

Talia knew she should call a halt. But the growing desire in him sang to her soul in a way which was tantalizing in its unfamiliarity. It was as if she'd never really been kissed before, never known the full complexities of a woman's response. Which was ridiculous. She was thirty years old, she reminded herself, she'd been engaged to be married, thought herself in love . . .

"This afternoon when I found you at the pool it was all I could do not to reach out and touch you like this."

Talia's senses shimmered as Kane's hand closed inevitably and with teasing gentleness over one full breast. It seemed to swell at his touch.

"You're just not built the way a blackmailer should be built, honey," he growled in sexy humor as he buried his lips in the curve of her throat. "You're too soft, too warm, too inviting."

"Please, Kane," Talia heard herself say as she trembled. "Don't keep calling me that!"

"You don't like the sound of blackmail?" he taunted softly. "But it's so effective, darling. Didn't it get you exactly what you wanted?"

"Yes, but I don't . . . I want . . ."

She broke off on a passionate little cry as he began stroking the silk-covered tip of her breast. The lacy bra beneath was not sufficient to dull the impact of the caress. Talia felt her nipple harden almost painfully in response, its outline easily felt through the thin layers of fabric. He must know beyond any shadow of a doubt what he was doing to her!

"Like small ripe berries," Kane rasped, his voice deepening with undisguised male pleasure. "I want to see them, taste them . . ."

Talia shut her eyes convulsively, pressing her face into his jacket as he slid the ruffled silk off one shoulder. Her fingers splayed across his chest in reaction as he bared the upper curve of her breasts. She took a primitive, very female delight in the sound of his sharp, husky exclamation of desire and her nails dug into the fabric of his shirt beneath his coat.

"Undress me, honey. I want to feel your hands on my skin. I want to feel your softness."

Kane released her momentarily to shrug out of the jacket, letting the expensive material slide, unheeded, to the floor. Then, as if they had a will of their own, Talia's fingers were fumbling with the buttons of the crisp, white shirt. Excitement rose in her. She was experiencing the most incredible eagerness to blaze enticing paths through the curling hair on his broad chest. For some crazy reason she was entranced by the bold red shade of that hair.

She felt the clasp of her bra being released just as she reached her goal.

"Oh, Kane!"

His name was a soft cry far back in her throat as he cupped her fullness. Desire flamed thickly in the bottom of her stomach as his thumbs glided gently across the hardened tips of her soft orbs.

She responded in kind, finding the flat, male nipples with her fingertips. When he shuddered and sank his teeth into the lobe of her ear, she bent her head to touch the tip of her tongue where her fingers had been.

"My God, Talia. Do you know what you're doing to me?" he said, his voice thick with desire. "Is this what you did to Hazelton? No wonder he . . ."

Talia froze, a violent coldness washing out the flames of passion in one awful wave. She stepped back so abruptly Kane's hands fell away in surprise.

"Get out of here!"

His jaw tightened as he stared at her. She could almost feel the still-high desire in him urging him to grab her close once more and set about finishing what had been begun.

"What the hell's the matter with you?" he grated, taking a menacing step forward.

"I asked you to leave, Kane."

Turning away from the anger and passion warring in his face, Talia fumbled shakily with the bodice of the apricot silk. Desperately she struggled for control of her voice and her clothing.

"It was Hazelton's name, wasn't it?" he ground out behind her. "I shouldn't have brought it up so soon."

"You mean you shouldn't have brought it up *ever*!" She nearly snarled, whirling on him like a small, cornered tigress. Realizing how little self-control she had at that moment, Talia closed her eyes, striving for great calm.

"Never mind," she finally managed tightly. "It's not important. Just something I don't care to discuss. I shouldn't have lost my temper, but perhaps it was for the best." Her lashes rose abruptly to reveal her near-gold eyes. "Will you please leave? Things were going much too far . . ."

The hard mouth softened almost indulgently as Kane

44

slowly began to do up the buttons of his shirt and stuff the ends into the waistband of his close-fitting slacks.

He made a disturbingly intimate picture standing in the middle of her room, casually adjusting his clothing. The faintly tousled chestnut hair, the fading heat of passion in the green eyes, the shirt collar he chose to leave open all seemed to be affecting her strangely. Talia had a horrifying impulse to withdraw her command, tell him she hadn't truly meant it.

"You're entitled to your opinion, of course," he drawled, bending to scoop up his jacket and toss it carelessly over one shoulder. "Personally, I think we were just getting started." He turned and strode toward the door. "I'll call you as soon as I hear anything from South America," he volunteered sardonically just before letting himself out. And then he was gone.

Talia stared for a long, shaky moment at the closed door. She should never have let that good-night kiss get so out of hand. A little dazed, she made a stab at understanding her shockingly strong reaction to a man she had every reason to dislike.

He was not only not her type; he was the very essence of all she had come to resent so fiercely three years ago.

Wasn't he?

CHAPTER THREE

He didn't call until nearly noon the next day and Talia jumped at the phone, grabbing the receiver before the first ring had finished.

"How nice to know you're sitting at home waiting for my calls!" Kane mocked as she managed a polite greeting.

"Did you hear anything?" She reacted to the taunting in his voice with brittle tartness.

"I'm crushed. You mean it wasn't me you were dying to talk to? You're only interested in the news I might have?"

"I can't afford to be interested in you," Talia retorted, a smile lifting her mouth. "You proved that last night."

"You mean because I'm so damn sexy you might lose your head?"

"I mean because you drink '73 Cabernets, order clams Bordelaise and chateaubriand and the most expensive dessert on the menu, and then make me pay for it!"

"Oh, that," he murmured nonchalantly. "I thought it

46

best to start off as I mean to go on. I didn't want you getting the idea I'm a cheap date."

"Kane," Talia began warningly.

"Okay, okay. Don't get too excited. I haven't heard anything yet."

"Damn!" Talia muttered.

"But don't give up hope. I sent the cable to someone who used to work for us down there. He's probably doing some checking. Give it another day or two."

Talia frowned into the phone. "You think there's a chance of turning up a lead?"

"Who knows? The trail's a little cold, you'll have to admit. It was four years ago that Westbrook worked for Energy Interface and he was only on the payroll a few weeks. Look, it's almost lunchtime and if you've been sitting around that hotel room waiting for this call all morning you're probably stir-crazy."

"How did you guess?"

"Intuition. I'd be doing the same in your shoes. I'll be by in a few minutes to take you to lunch."

"Who's paying?" Talia demanded suspiciously.

"I'm feeling generous. I'll charge you off as a business expense. That reminds me, I'll have to check with my accountant to see if blackmail expenses are deductible . . ."

Talia didn't wait for him to finish. She hung up the phone in his ear.

Knowing Kane would arrive dressed for the office, Talia decided to wear the pleated skirt of her wheat-colored suit. She chose another blouse she had brought along, a silk crêpe de chine print in cinnamon and gold paisley. After a long look at the suit jacket, she opted to leave it behind. It was just too warm and, besides, it was Kane who had

47

to go back to an office environment, not her. That thought sparked others which were depressing. Once her whole wardrobe had been geared to the executive suite.

But even Kane, it seemed, made a few concessions to the heat of the September sun. He arrived at her door minus his jacket and without a tie. The white shirt was strictly tailored, but the collar was open and the contrast against his tanned skin gave him a buccaneering quality which was not lost on Talia. She smiled up at him a little warily as she opened the door.

"Don't look at me like that, honey," he drawled, "I told you I'm paying for lunch."

"Sorry. Once burned . . ."

"You deserved it. Ready?"

"I'd go out with Attila the Hun if it meant getting out of this hotel room!"

"Careful, your flattery will go to my head," he growled, slanting a green, appraising glance down at her as she walked beside him toward the parking lot.

"Where are we going?"

"Old Sacramento. Remember it?"

Talia nodded, recalling the restoration work that had been going on in a twenty-eight-acre section near the river. The colorful atmosphere of Sacramento in the 1850s and 1860s had been re-created and the historic buildings now housed some of the city's most unique restaurants and shops.

"They've done a good job with it," Kane went on as he stopped beside a gleaming red Lotus and fitted a key into the lock. "Plank sidewalks, old-fashioned awnings, stagecoaches, and an occasional gunfight at the railroad depot. Great background."

Talia managed to wrench her eyes off the Lotus long

48

enough to glance at him inquiringly. "Great background for what?"

"I'm not going to tell you or you might refuse to go out with me, even for a free lunch!"

It wasn't until the Lotus had been carefully wedged into a tiny slip of a parking space near the restaurant Kane had chosen that the truth came out.

"Oh, no!" Talia wailed in mock dismay as the elegant little Nikon camera was lovingly removed from its hiding place and slung across Kane's chest. A leather bag which was undoubtedly full of film, lenses, and related paraphernalia followed.

"You have your hobby, I have mine," Kane declared defensively, opening the car door and assisting her out. "At least I can count on results with mine!"

"I'd have thought you would have already taken all the pictures anyone could want of Old Sacramento by now. You've been in the area for years!"

"But I haven't got any pictures with you in them," he pointed out cheerfully, pushing her lightly in the direction of a California-style Mexican restaurant.

"Don't expect me to model!" she told him waspishly, hiding a smile at the sight he made strung with camera equipment. "You look like one of those tourists getting off the tour bus over there!" She nodded toward a plush coach dispensing an assortment of passengers, most with cameras around their necks.

"I'll try not to embarrass you unduly," he said placatingly, leading her into the restaurant.

The light banter continued over a lunch of crunchy tostadas and tortilla chips served in the cool atmosphere of early California. Afterward, Kane seemed in no par-

49

ticular hurry to rush back to the office and suggested they browse through some of the nearby shops.

"Hold it right there," he ordered suddenly just as Talia was about to enter an antique store.

She paused, her tawny head with its neat twist catching the noonday sun, one hand braced on the doorframe.

"What's the matter?" She turned her head slightly to look at him and, too late, realized the Nikon was pointed in her direction. Her mouth quirked wryly. "You didn't give me a chance to smile!" she protested as the shutter clicked.

"I liked that look of idle interest," he told her airily, letting the camera fall back into place across his chest. "Natural shots are always the best," he added with a meaningful grin.

"Don't get any ideas. I don't do cheesecake!"

"Honey, I'm no leering amateur," he defended. "I take my photography very seriously. It's an art!"

They made the round of the various shops and Talia gradually grew accustomed to having Kane suddenly leap out in front of her to snap another photograph. She was posed on the steps of an opulent private railroad car in the railroad museum, caught in profile as she petted the nose of a bored-looking horse pulling a wagon full of tourists, and shot unawares as she deliberated over the purchase of a straw hat.

"I hate to call a halt, but I suppose I really should be getting back to the office," Kane finally announced regretfully as he closed the camera case.

"Perhaps there will have been a response to the cable by the time you get back," Talia said with hopeful speculation.

"It's nice to know exactly what my appeal is for you,"

50

he grumbled, escorting her gently into the front seat of the Lotus. "You have a way of driving a knife through my fragile ego, Talia Haywood."

"I'm sorry," Talia said abruptly and genuinely contrite. She caught his hand as it rested on the door's edge and looked up at him earnestly. "I really did enjoy lunch and touring the shops. It's been a lovely afternoon."

He smiled but there was a cool greenness in his eyes as he lifted the hand that had touched his and bared her wrist. He said nothing, dropping a small, highly charged kiss on the soft, sensitive skin at the base of her palm. Talia felt a tiny, sensual shock go through her system. Why, oh, why, did she react so to this man?

He drove her back to the hotel, saying little en route. When he pulled into the front entrance, she climbed out and turned politely to thank him for lunch.

"I'll pick you up around seven for dinner," he said quietly, ignoring her thanks.

She stared at him a little uncertainly, sensing that the easy banter had disappeared. Had she really offended him that badly with her remark about an answer to the cable?

"That's . . . that's very nice of you, but not necessary," she began quickly, anxious to let him off the hook in case he was feeling obligated for some obscure reason. Not that it was easy to imagine this man feeling obligated to anyone, especially the woman who had threatened to black-mail him.

"You're not doing anything else, are you? Or had you planned to look up an old boyfriend or two?" he demanded with a trace of pure sarcasm.

Talia withdrew a step or so from the car as if he'd made some move to reach out and hit her. "No," she told him starkly. "I won't be looking up any old boyfriends."

"Fine. I'll see you at seven."

She watched him ease the Lotus expertly out onto the street and for a sad, angry moment, memories of one particular old boyfriend came back to haunt her. Where was Richard now? How long had it taken him to find a new, uncompromised fiancée? she wondered bitterly.

Compromised. It was an old-fashioned word to describe what had happened to her during her climb to the top. There weren't many ways a modern woman could be compromised, but it was still possible in the upper echelons of the corporate world. More than one career had been ruined. And, just as in the old days, it was the woman who suffered.

Talia took a grip on her emotions. With the ease of practice, she forced aside the memories of Richard Fairfax, the bright, young lawyer to whom she had been engaged three years earlier. Richard had had his sights set on California politics. He didn't need a wife who had been accused of trying to sleep her way into a vice-presidency. And she no longer needed Richard, Talia thought grimly. But some of the anger remained.

She swam again that afternoon, unable to maintain the vigil by the telephone the way she had that morning. The heat of the day required quenching and besides, she had waited so long for her answers to the mystery of Justin Westbrook, she could wait a little longer. Reminding herself that Kane's cable probably wouldn't turn up anything useful anyway, Talia made herself concentrate on an espionage thriller as she sat beneath an umbrella at poolside.

That evening when she opened the door to him, Kane was quick to satisfy the silent query on her face.

"Sorry," he said laconically, stepping into the hotel

52

room. "No word yet. You'll have to spend another day or so, I'm afraid."

He tossed her an offhand smile, his gaze moving over her figure. The green eyes gleamed as he took in the graceful, dolman-sleeved dress. The exotic, flower-printed challis clung to her body with beguiling softness, outlining her gentle shape as she moved. The color mix of purple and gold and red was lush and exotic. A curving neckline framed the small beaded necklace that closely circled her throat.

Talia was glad she had dressed well for the evening. There was an understated, masculine elegance in Kane's tan jacket and dark brown slacks. He wore a chocolate brown shirt open at the throat, which emphasized the raffish air that emanated from him.

"I'm not sure how much longer I should stay," she mused as they walked toward the Lotus. "I've told my boss I'm taking a couple of days' vacation and he's arranged to have someone cover for me, but . . ."

"A very understanding sort of boss," Kane murmured as he helped her into the car.

Talia flicked him a wary look and decided it would be safest if she kept the conversation directed away from herself. She definitely did not want Kane Sebastian exploring the topic of understanding bosses. He was bound to get back to the subject of Hazelton eventually if she allowed him to do so. And somehow this evening promised to be pleasant. She didn't want it spoiled by any probing of the past.

"Have you always been your own boss?" she inquired coolly as Kane guided the car through the city streets.

"Ever since I started Energy Interface Systems a few years ago," he confirmed equably, apparently content to answer her questions. Talia seized on the opportunity, suddenly aware of how deeply curious she was becoming about this man.

"And before that?"

"I worked for a lot of different people in a lot of different places," he shrugged. "Mostly oil-field development stuff."

"An engineer?" She hazarded a guess.

"A roustabout," he corrected with a wry grin. "A lot of rough, sweaty, hard work. The engineers got to work in air-conditioned trailers. The benefits of a higher education, I suppose."

"Something tells me you're making more now than most of them ever will."

"Is that a polite way of asking to see my bank balance?"

Talia turned a furious shade of red, appalled at herself. "Don't be ridiculous. I only mean that you're obviously a successful, self-made man," she said stiffly.

"You're not going to hold my, er, plebeian background against me?" He chuckled.

"The only thing that matters in the end in the business world is success or failure. You're obviously a success," Talia replied quietly, taking him seriously. She'd had a good education and it hadn't helped her at all in the battle for corporate survival. A good education might provide an entrée into that world, but it didn't keep one alive in it.

"I have many of the things I wanted in life," he agreed slowly.

"But not all?"

"Having it all would be a fate worse than death, wouldn't it?" he suggested lightly, pulling into the parking lot of a excellent Italian restaurant that Talia remembered from her earlier stay in Sacramento. She and Richard had come here . . .

"You mean you thrive on challenge," she said in response to his rhetorical question.

"Is that so bad?"

"It is when carried to extremes," Talia told him seriously. "People get hurt when the need to feed on a challenge becomes destructive."

He parked the car and turned in the seat to study her intently. "Who gets hurt, Talia? The one who responds to the challenge or the people around him?"

She sensed the urgency in his question and wished she'd kept her mouth shut. But she lifted her chin and answered him anyway. "The people around him. It's very difficult to work for an excitement freak, you know," she added calmly, opening her car door.

Instantly he was out of his side, coming around to take her arm.

"Excitement freak," he repeated thoughtfully as they walked toward the restaurant. "Is that a term from your class lectures?"

"I am constantly warning my students to be on the lookout for that particular personality quirk, both in themselves and in others," Talia said deliberately.

"And the definition?"

"An excitement freak is someone who thrives so much on challenge and excitement in his or her environment that he or she will deliberately keep a situation in turmoil just to create a constant state of emotional high. For a lot of corporate executives excitement is addictive. When they run out of sufficient challenge in the normal course of events, they create it."

"How?" Kane looked fascinated as he led her through

the doors and into the darkened interior of the plush restaurant lobby.

She shrugged. "By having affairs, by maneuvering against other people who may someday be a threat, by stirring up crisis situations that call for mastery and decisiveness. Lots of ways."

The deferential politeness with which they were shown to their table told Talia that Kane was a most welcome client. There was a subdued flurry of activity which resulted in her being carefully seated, a bottle of chilled Chenin Blanc ordered, and a huge leather menu placed in her hand.

"Does your expertise tell you I'm one of those types?" Kane asked politely once they had been left alone. He regarded her over the expanse of a gleaming white tablecloth, green eyes reflecting the flame of the candlelight.

"I don't know you well enough to say," she admitted honestly.

"Let me try a bit of self-analysis then," he said smoothly as the wine arrived.

She watched him go through the ritual of tasting and accepting the light golden liquid, wondering what he was about to reveal about himself. She had meant it when she'd told him she didn't know if he qualified as an excitement freak. There was no doubt that he enjoyed a challenge and yesterday she would have said he probably was the type who constantly had to be proving himself, testing himself against all comers. But tonight she wasn't so sure. He had backed down in the face of her poor blackmail attempt and he had seemed genuinely relaxed and enthusiastic with his photography hobby. Kane Sebastian was proving a little more complex than she would have first thought.

Talia picked up her glass, swirling it automatically as she prepared to sip. Over the rim she met Kane's considering gaze and waited.

"Let me see," he murmured. "Am I an excitement freak? Well, I don't go around stirring up crisis situations at work. I count a good day as one that runs smoothly and calmly toward an established goal. I don't deliberately precipitate a flurry of decision-making situations. They occur frequently enough without creating them! I have no need to maneuver against rivals because I'm already the boss," he went on simply.

Talia smiled slightly at that. "A good point."

"And given the amount of time that has elapsed since my last full-fledged affair, I think I can safely say I don't look for challenge in my women." He smiled directly at her as he made that last statement, nodding almost imperceptibly as the color rose in her cheeks.

"Yes, well, congratulations," she managed blithely, trying to ignore the very definite challenge that was gleaming at her from the depths of those green, candlelit pools he called eyes. "Perhaps you've escaped the trap."

"Don't you want to hear how long it's been since my last affair?"

"Kane!"

"Not a topic of conversation for the dinner table?"

"Definitely not!"

"I consider a good affair to be very much like a good business arrangement," he observed as if she hadn't spoken. "Both parties want something from the other and come together in order to obtain it. What would you want out of an affair, Talia Haywood?"

"If you don't change the topic of this conversation this

instant, I will be leaving you to philosophize with an empty chair!" she gritted.

"A sure way to kill a nice evening," he lamented, picking up the menu.

"Stone dead," she agreed, seeing that she had won the small skirmish. The relief brought a tiny hint of smugness to her smile as she picked up her own menu, a smugness that disappeared an instant later as a far-too-familiar male voice hailed her from nearby.

"Talia! For goodness' sake! What are you doing here?"

The warmth of the evening dissipated from the atmosphere around her as Talia lifted her eyes slowly to the tall, good-looking man standing at her elbow. She knew what she would see even before she got as far as the carefully styled black hair and the smile that came too easily to the handsome features. Dark eyes met her upturned amber ones with an open enthusiasm and genuine light that made her almost ill. It was so completely phony. All of it. Richard Fairfax, she thought, not for the first time, really would make a fine politician. How could she have ever believed in the warmth and integrity promised in those dark eyes?

"Hello, Richard," she said quietly.

"Talia, it's great to see you. I couldn't believe it when I walked in a few minutes ago and caught sight of you. I'm here with some campaign workers tonight and I had to come over and say hello." Without waiting for an introduction, Richard Fairfax extended his hand to Kane. "Richard Fairfax. You're Kane Sebastian, aren't you? Head of Energy Interface Systems? I'm happy to have the chance to meet you. You've done a lot to open up Sacramento to overseas business opportunities."

Kane accepted the handshake with thin politeness.

Talia could almost see the watchful hostility in him. It was flowing across the table in waves and she wondered at it. "You're a friend of Talia's?"

"Oh, Talia and I were once very close, weren't we, darling?" Richard said with a barely concealed hint of intimacy that infuriated her. She knew exactly what he was doing. Under cover of superficial civility, Richard was letting Kane know he'd once had a claim on her. It was an unsubtle one-upmanship which was neatly staged to make him the dominant male in the small scene. She could feel her anger rising in a red tide. Richard hadn't wanted her three years ago after she'd been humiliated, yet here he was perfectly willing to embarrass her for the sake of his ego.

"No," she said with stark simplicity. "Looking back on it, I don't think you could say we really were very close at all. Good evening, Richard. You'll excuse me, I'm sure."

She turned to face Kane, willing him to follow her lead and experiencing the most compelling flash of gratitude when he did so.

"You heard the lady, Fairfax," Kane said very quietly.

Richard's dark eyes narrowed as he studied Talia's averted features. "Of course," he said coolly, walking away toward a table full of people in the corner of the room. She knew he was angry and it gave her a certain satisfaction.

"Thank you," she said honestly to Kane in the small silence that followed.

"My pleasure," he returned sardonically. "An old boyfriend?"

"I was engaged to him," she admitted bleakly.

"I see."

To her surprise Kane didn't press the point. Instead he concentrated on exerting the charm he had demonstrated the previous evening. Within an astonishingly short period of time Talia was once again enjoying herself, Richard Fairfax all but forgotten.

The prosciutto and melon appetizer was followed by a lightly dressed salad and a perfectly cooked veal piccata. The chocolate mousse might not have been, strictly speaking, Italian, but it was the perfect ending to a meal that went down as nicely as the conversation.

Talia was feeling that marvelously hazy, slightly floating sensation that accompanies evenings that will be remembered when Kane left her in the lobby to fetch the car.

"But I walked in from the car," she protested when he told her kindly to wait for him.

"But I don't feel like carrying you out to it now." He grinned and bent to drop a quick kiss on the tip of her nose.

"Are you implying I'm tipsy?" she demanded with a low laugh. She wasn't. She was just feeling happy. Happier than she'd felt in a long time.

"I wouldn't think of implying any such thing. Just wait here like a good girl and I'll be right back with the car," Kane instructed.

Talia sat down obediently as he made his way out the door and into the night. She was smiling at the closed door, wondering about the marvelously warm sense of expectation she was experiencing when Richard Fairfax once more stepped in to ruin the evening.

"Oh, Richard. I'd forgotten you were here," Talia observed coldly.

"How long are you going to be in town, Talia?"

"A couple of days. I'm here on business," she told him repressively.

"I can see. With the head of Energy Interface Systems, no less. He's an important man, Talia. You could do an old friend a favor by putting in a good word for me," he said encouragingly. "He wields some influence in the business community and I'm trying to establish a reputation as being a friend of business."

"Don't be ridiculous, Richard. I wouldn't go out of my way to help you if my life depended on it!"

"Don't be so hasty, darling," he soothed arrogantly, reaching out to flick her cheek with a careless finger. "You've obviously got a good thing going for yourself with him. He's a hell of a catch and I wouldn't want to spoil it for you!"

"How?" She glared at him, thoroughly disgusted. How could she have ever thought herself in love with this man?

"Simple enough. All I'd have to do is remind him of that little mess three years ago over at Darius & Darnell. Somehow I don't think Kane Sebastian would want to go beyond an affair with the woman who figured in that scandal. If you have any hopes of getting him to marry you, you'd better make sure he doesn't find out you've got a reputation for sleeping your way into promotions!"

Stunned, Talia got to her feet, shaking with her fury. "How dare you?" she breathed. "How *dare* you!"

"Something wrong?"

She whirled at the sound of Kane's quietly menacing voice behind her. Unthinkingly she stepped toward him as if toward protection. "No, Kane, nothing is wrong," she got out through clenched teeth. "But Richard, here, has a little friendly warning for you. A sort of man-to-man piece of advice."

"Thanks, but no thanks," Kane said calmly, his fingers closing over the hand Talia had wrapped around his sleeve.

"Oh, no," she protested, her voice tight with fury. "This is for your own good. Richard is running for office, you see, and he'd like your help. He'd like it so badly that he's just finished threatening to tell you about my involvement in that mess at Darius & Darnell if I don't agree to put in a good word for him with you! He's concerned, you understand, that if you were to find out I have a reputation for trying to sleep my way up in this world you might not want to marry me. You might only want an affair with me!"

She felt the sinewy muscles in his forearm tighten as she talked. Kane's whole body was like a coiled spring beneath her touch, but when he spoke his deep voice was lazy and filled with a mocking amusement.

"Thank you for your concern, Fairfax," he drawled, "but the simple fact of the matter is, I couldn't care less what happened three years ago. I will be marrying Talia, but don't expect an invitation to the wedding. Just to show you what a fair man I am, however, I will give you a little warning in return. Stay away from Talia in the future or I will not only fail to contribute to your campaign fund—I must admit I hadn't planned to, anyway—but I will take you apart piece by piece. Is that understood?"

Richard, his gaze furious, his cosmetically tanned face flushed with anger and humiliation, turned on his heel and left. Talia needed no treatise on management power techniques to understand that Kane had demolished the younger man with consummate ease.

"Normally," she declared with relish as they walked out to the waiting car, "I do not approve of social lies, but in this instance I must admit there was a certain pleasure in hearing you tell Richard you were going to marry me regardless of that business at Darius & Darnell! The nerve of that man! I can't imagine what I ever saw in him. To think that three years ago I was in tears because of him." She shook her head. "I suppose he'll realize soon enough we're not being married, but just the same, it was fun to see his face this evening when you told him to go to hell!"

He threw her a strange glance as he started the Lotus. "Just part of the service."

"What service? Oh, you mean the service I'm black-mailing you into rendering." She chuckled, struck by the humor of the situation. "I must admit, tonight you went above and beyond the duties of the average victim. Just for that, I'll buy you dinner tomorrow night if I'm still in town."

"A most magnanimous blackmailer."

"I try to bring a certain level of sophistication to the job." She laughed. "Oh, Kane, thank you. I really mean it. I never thought I'd get the chance to see Richard in such a humiliating position!"

There was an enigmatic lift to his lips as he drove her back to the hotel, but he said nothing until he had walked her to the door of her room.

"About tomorrow night," he began, taking her into his arms.

"Yes?" she whispered agreeably, quite content to stand in the circle of his embrace.

"Thank you for your generous offer of dinner, but I had other plans."

"Oh!" She started to pull away, embarrassed at her own assumption.

He held her firmly. "I had other plans for *us*," he explained smoothly. "I'll pick you up at the same time as I did this evening, okay? Wear something casual."

"Casual," she repeated carefully, trying to fathom the expression in his eyes.

"Casual. Good night, sweet blackmailer."

He kissed her slowly, lingering over the warmth of her mouth as if it were dessert to the pleasant meal that had gone before. But he made no move to follow her into the hotel room.

As Talia locked the door behind him she realized with a shaft of surprise just how bereft she felt.

CHAPTER FOUR

"I see you meant it when you said casual." Talia smiled the next evening when she opened the door to Kane. He was wearing a plaid Western shirt with the sleeves rolled up on his strong forearms and the collar undone. A pair of snug-fitting jeans rode low on his hips and were finished off with well-worn boots. A wide leather belt girded the lean waist, the buckle engraved with a Western motif. He could have just walked in off the range, a saddle slung over one shoulder.

He threw her a lazy, appraising grin, surveying her narrow white pants and rakish khaki fly-front blouse. "I have hidden depths."

"So I see. An alter ego?"

"Everyone in the business world needs a few unrelated identities. Keeps you sane."

Talia blinked, knowing he meant the comment as a humorous one but struck, nevertheless, with the perception behind it. The more she learned about this man, the less he seemed like the stereotyped corporate wolf she had first imagined.

"Ready?" he asked, glancing around the hotel room. "Sorry there was no word back from South America today," he added solicitously. "Did you spend the whole day sitting around here?"

"No, I went shopping in the mall downtown and swimming in the afternoon," Talia told him, remembering how she had felt less anxious about possible news from South America. Somehow the approaching evening with Kane had become more important. She had been looking for Justin Westbrook a long time and would continue to do so, but Kane Sebastian was a far more immediate and tantalizing reality this evening. "Where are we going?"

"My place," he told her on the way out to the Lotus. "If you're nice to me, I might invite you in to see my slides."

"The problem in dating photographers is that they generally mean just that," she retorted. "I warn you, I have a limited attention span."

"I'll try to keep you amused with my informative narrative."

The warmth in his eyes and the affection in his voice flitted enticingly along Talia's nerves. She felt like a cat being stroked every time he looked at her. Any doubts she might have had about dining in the intimacy of his home vanished almost as soon as they appeared. She was more than mildly attracted to the man and she knew it. She was rapidly becoming drawn to him in a way that should have struck her as dangerous but seemed, instead, totally natural, almost fated.

Kane chose the freeway out of town, leaving the city behind and eventually turning off on a two-lane road that headed roughly southeast. Around them the flat, agriculturally rich farmland of California's central valley lay cooling under a waning sun.

"Don't tell me you live on a ranch!" Talia remarked, taking another look at the boots and jeans while surveying the passing scenery.

He laughed. "Haven't got time for ranching. I own a condominium in one of the country club developments. Disappointed?"

"Not really. I'm allergic to hay." She chuckled, relaxing back into the leather seat. "A country club cowboy, hmm?"

"A small personal rebellion, I'm afraid. I don't even play golf. My neighbors don't understand me."

"I can imagine," she commiserated. "You don't exactly look as if you would fit into the country club set at the moment. Although," she went on thoughtfully, "in your normal work attire . . ."

"As I said, a man of many aspects," he observed blandly.

"Why did you buy a country club home if you don't enjoy golf and the atmosphere that goes with it?"

He shot her a quick, slanting glance. "Because I'm going to make a killing on the condo in two years. It was a hell of a business opportunity. I got it after the developer had been hit by the housing recession. Picked it up for a song."

"I should have guessed. A businessman to your fingertips."

He shrugged. "And a photographer," he reminded her.

"When did you take up that hobby?"

"This year," he grinned. "Can't you tell that I've still got a novice's enthusiasm?"

"I've always wondered what photography buffs do with all the pictures that must accumulate!"

"Stick 'em in drawers, make slides out of them, and file them, throw away the absolutely rotten ones. And show the best to visiting ladies, of course," he concluded lightly.

The rolling fairways of a deliciously green golf course came into view and Kane guided the Lotus through guarded gates and up a winding drive lined with elegant homes and condominiums.

He parked the Lotus in front of a gracious condominium designed with a modern flair tempered by the Spanish touch. Inside, walls of windows took advantage of the cool, green view of the golf course. Vaulted ceilings, a richly tiled entrance hall, and a plush, tan carpet provided the setting for the furnishings of brass, glass, and leather. A successful businessman's home, Talia thought as she trailed a fingertip along the edge of a coffee-colored leather chair-back. Suitable for entertaining. She found herself wondering how many women had been entertained in these surroundings.

"So you went swimming this afternoon?" Kane asked equably as he mixed tall, cool tequila sunrises in the well-appointed kitchen.

"Oh, yes," Talia smiled, accepting her drink. "It was too hot to do anything else and I couldn't stand to sit in that hotel room waiting for a call from you!"

He winced. "Am I losing my boyish appeal?" He led her out onto the landscaped patio where cool evening breezes were beginning to refresh the atmosphere.

Talia ignored his question, asking politely instead, "What about you? What did you do all afternoon?"

"I," he said, dropping his bombshell with negligent finesse, "spent most of it at the public library."

Talia looked up from stirring her ice with her finger. "The library! What on earth were you doing there?"

He met her eyes levelly. "Going through some old newspaper accounts of a three-year-old scandal." The easy-going humor was gone. The emerald eyes met and held hers in green chains, daring her to get up and run.

That was exactly what she wanted to do, Talia acknowledged in harsh self-condemnation. Run.

"Why would you want to do that?" she whispered tightly.

"Maybe because I was growing more and more curious about my lady blackmailer. You want to tell me about what happened three years ago?"

"Not particularly," she grated, her features composing themselves into the cool, aloof facade she adopted instinctively whenever the subject came up. "If you took the trouble to read the papers, you know all there is to know."

Her words were as cool as her composure, but inside the anger was simmering once more close to the surface. How dare he reopen those old wounds? He'd brought her out here, miles from the city, treated her as if they were enjoying a casual date, and then hit her with this!

"I know what was being said about you and Hazelton. I know you resigned because of the not-so-subtle accusations and I know you left town. What I want to hear is your side of the story."

Talia's fingers tightened around the frosty glass and her soft mouth firmed. She could sense the unyielding demand in Kane; she knew he would not cease pressing her until she gave him the answers. The strange part was that a portion of her wanted to tell him the whole sordid tale. But that would mean admitting her own weakness and she

69

wasn't at all sure she could risk baring her soul to this man.

"The story is mine and I do not wish to go into it," she said quietly.

"Then let me guess," Kane said, equally quietly, his face hard and intent as he leaned forward, elbows resting on his knees, the glass cradled between his palms. "You were bright, educated, and on your way to that vice-presidency when someone named Derek Hazelton stepped in your path and said he could make your fast track even faster if you were nice to him. Right so far?"

"You sound as if you may have made the offer a few times yourself!" she was stung into retorting.

He ignored the accusation. "The big question is, what did you say to Hazelton at that point, Talia?"

Talia rose to her feet in a swift, agitated movement. "I told him to go to hell!" she flared. Turning her back on him, she braced herself against the railing and gazed blindly out over the darkening golf course. "What do you think I told him?" she concluded bitterly.

"Life must have gotten rough after that," he observed behind her in an enigmatic tone.

She lifted her chin. "Very rough." She took a deep breath, remembering. "Hazelton was my boss. He began bombarding me with incredible quantities of purely clerical work. He excluded me from important meetings. He kept vital information from me and then made accusations of incompetence when I made mistakes because I lacked that information. He ruined crucial business relationships I had established. God! There are so many ways of punishing a manager who reports to you. I hadn't even dreamed people could do things like that to other people. Not in real life."

"So you saw your career going down the drain and Hazelton gave you another chance, right?"

Talia bit her lip. "He let me know my problems could all be solved with a weekend in San Francisco." She had been nothing more than an amusing challenge for Derek Hazelton. When she'd resisted, he'd casually crushed her whole career.

"A weekend with him."

"Yes."

"And you said no, still believing you could get that promotion on your own merits?"

"Naive, wasn't I?" she gritted. "As the promotion drew closer, rumors started to circulate. The board of directors got wind of them and after that, the newspapers. They had a field day with it!"

"I saw," Kane admitted.

"I tried to explain what had happened, but no one listened. Even . . ." She broke off on a strangled sob that she forced back down her throat.

"Even who, Talia?" The deep voice was soft now, coaxing, persuading, soothing.

"Even my fiancé," she whispered. "Oh, Richard claimed he believed me, but he pointed out that he was planning a career in politics. He really shouldn't be burdened with a compromised wife!"

"So the engagement was broken off?"

"Naturally." Talia had regained control of herself once more. The worst was over. Proudly she swung around to face Kane, amber eyes glinting in the patio light. "That's it. End of story. Still going to feed me dinner?" she managed with savage flippancy. "You don't have to worry about being seen with me, you know. Just like in the old days, it's not the man who suffers from the gossip."

He was watching her with that enigmatic look she'd seen more than once in those emerald eyes, as if he were analyzing and judging. Condemning?

"Do you," he asked, without a change of expression, "like your steaks rare or medium rare? I refuse to cook good meat to the well-done stage on general principles."

She blinked, taken offguard for an instant. "Rare," she whispered after a long moment. "Very."

A slow grin slashed across his face as Kane got to his feet. "A woman after my own heart. Can I talk you into making the salad while I start the barbecue?"

Dazed, Talia nodded and followed him silently back into the kitchen. What did he think of her? Why had he pushed so hard for her side of the story? And why would a man, who must surely be hectically busy at the office, take the afternoon off to read old newspaper stories at the public library?

"I trust you'll make all the appropriately approving comments on my brilliant photographic essays," Kane warned some time later as they dined by candlelight on the patio.

"That depends," she temporized, finishing her melt-in-the-mouth cut-with-a-fork steak. "Am I going to have to sit through a lot of shots of Disneyland, the Pacific coastline, and ex-wives? Or are you into flowers?" she added quickly, regretting the implied question about ex-wives.

He looked up and snagged her glance. "No wives. I only took up photography a year ago and the one ex-wife was out of the picture, literally, a long time before that."

"Oh, well, in that case . . ." Talia began with determined airiness.

"She left me," he continued very deliberately, not

releasing Talia's eyes, "shortly after we were married, About the time it looked as if Energy Interface Systems might not make it. There were better prospects around and she found one. She went back to the Midwest with him and is now happily playing the role of corporate wife and hostess, I suppose."

"I'm . . . I'm sorry . . ."

"Why? I'm not. The marriage was a mistake," he declared calmly, collecting dishes into a pile which he then prepared to carry into the kitchen. "Mistakes are best put behind one. After one has drawn all pertinent lessons from them, of course," he added with a small smile.

"Did you draw the proper lessons?" she dared to ask, picking up the remainder of the dishes.

"I think so," he claimed modestly, setting his burden down in the red enamel sink. "I learned, for example, that I was looking for all the wrong things in a woman back in those days."

Talia realized she was waiting a little breathlessly for him to continue. She came up behind him and reached around to set her dishes beside his.

He wrapped a hand around the back of her neck and smiled with dangerous sensuality down into her upturned face. His thumb moved tantalizingly along the line of her jaw.

"I don't need a corporate hostess. And I don't need a social queen to grace the head of my table."

"What . . . what do you need?" she couldn't resist asking, her whole body filled with a strange tension.

"Now that question is a hell of a lot tougher to answer," he admitted. "But I'm working on it."

He bent his head to crush her lips gently with his own.

"Stick around," he concluded a moment later as he

73

reluctantly broke off the kiss, "and I should be able to give you a definitive answer by morning." The green eyes darkened with the beginnings of desire.

"No," she whispered, shaken by the willpower it took to reject the sexual invitation he was extending.

"Yes," he countered very softly.

She shook her head.

"We'll start with the slides," he said with an air of decisiveness.

Starting with his slides was, Talia decided later, the cleverest seduction approach he could possibly have used. Through the medium of his novice photography Kane Sebastian came across as very human, very unthreatening.

They sat together on the tan leather sofa, Kane's booted feet propped up beside hers on the coffee table, his arm draped comfortably around her shoulders. In his free hand he controlled the slide projector with a remote switch.

On the white wall opposite, one image after another danced on display as Kane delivered his narrative. Talia found herself laughing one minute and exclaiming over an unexpectedly beautiful shot the next.

"What happened there?" she demanded for the fifth time as a strange shot of a lake appeared on the wall. "What are all those funny colors on the side?"

"I was running out of film," he explained cheerfully. "That was the last shot in the camera. Anyhow, as I was saying, I got up at five thirty in the morning to catch that lake when it would be as smooth as glass. Look at it. Not a ripple, not a mark on its surface!"

"If you could see the entire surface, it would have been very effective." Talia laughed. "But with all those strange colors fading off to the side . . ."

"It's obvious you have no appreciation of the intricacies

of fine photography," he grumbled, clicking in the next slide. "Now this one you can't quarrel with," he declared triumphantly.

"It's beautiful, Kane." Talia's admiration was genuine. A simple flower shot, he had caught the morning dew on a rose in a huge close-up. "That one's worth framing."

"You think so?" He eyed it critically.

"Oh, yes. The colors are gorgeous. It would look terrific behind this couch," she told him enthusiastically.

"What about this one?" he demanded, clicking in another slide.

"It's all fuzzy!"

"I was trying to give it a sort of hazy glow—you know, setting a mood," he protested.

"Let's go on," Talia suggested firmly. "Ah. Now *that* I like. Too bad that car got into the background."

"Can't win 'em all," he told her philosophically. "Great texture, though, huh?"

"Fabulous," she grinned, not knowing what he was talking about.

Another click. Another slide.

"What in the world . . . ?" Talia leaned forward, trying to decipher the confused image on the screen.

"I tripped and the camera went off unaimed," he sighed. "I meant to take that one out."

"I don't know. That one has real possibilities," she told him thoughtfully. "Blown up and framed it would look like a work of modern art. Something out of the New York school, I should think."

"This is California," he reminded her stonily and went on to the next slide. "Now here's an interesting shot. I was on my way back from work late one evening this summer. I think I'll call it 'Sunset over the Capitol.' "

"Perhaps you could sell it to the governor. If he doesn't mind that strange shade of sunset."

"I was experimenting with my new filters," he remarked by way of explanation. "Now here's a nice series I took along the Sacramento River."

"Umm. I like those." She nodded.

In the intimate darkness of the room, one river scene after another shone brightly for a moment on the wall. It was very comfortable in some ways, Talia realized vaguely. Kane's arm around her felt warm and secure. Their shared laughter and comments would have made an outsider think they were a long-established couple. Unconsciously she allowed herself to snuggle a little closer to the warmth of his body.

"Is that one upside down?" she demanded mildly at one point.

"No, I always photograph historic buildings while standing on my head."

"I thought there would be a good explanation," she nodded, satisfied.

"Everyone's a critic," he groaned, sliding the hand that had been gently massaging Talia's shoulder along the curve of her throat and under her chin. Tilting her face upward, he turned his head to brush her lips with his own.

"Kane?"

"Hush," he soothed against her mouth, "I'm lining up a fantastic shot."

He forced her head back onto his shoulder, the hand under her chin holding her securely in place for his kiss. "I'd like a close-up of that mouth," he breathed huskily. "But I'm not sure I could do it justice with a camera."

"Oh, Kane!" With a small, shivering sound deep in her throat, Talia gave herself up to his kiss. She promised

76

herself it would be only a momentary surrender. She would only sip from the well of excitement he seemed to promise.

Tonight he seemed intent on taking his time. His mouth moved warmly on hers, creating a deepening intimacy that gently demanded admittance. His thumb slid upward from her chin to probe insistently at the corner of her mouth until her lips flowered open.

With a groan of growing passion, Kane was inside, invading her soft inner warmth. Talia felt the uncurling tendril of desire deep in her body and her fingertips crossed the expanse of his chest to the back of his neck. There they began toying with the thickness of his chestnut hair, delighting in its unexpected softness. It was like running her fingers through silky fire.

On the wall opposite them the last slide to be shown blazed forth to an uncaring audience. The soft whirr of the fan in the slide projector was the only other sound in the room, a backdrop for the gentle cries of longing Kane drew forth from Talia's lips.

Slowly, inevitably, he eased her back against the cushions until she lay beneath him, pinned by one blue-jeaned leg across her thighs.

"I could get addicted to the little sounds you make when you start to come alive under my hands," he growled hoarsely into her throat. "And the way your body trembles when I touch you."

"I didn't intend . . . I never meant . . ." Her voice broke off on a sigh as he began unfastening the buttons of her blouse.

"I know, honey, I know. But I want you so much. I've been wanting you all day. I couldn't get you out of my head!"

77

As if to punish her a little for invading his thoughts, Kane nipped sensuously at the tip of her ear. When she tried to turn her head in defense, he encircled her throat with gentle fingers, holding her still. Then he soothed the small wound with the tip of his tongue until she shivered once more beneath his weight.

Her blouse was magically open, freed from the waistband of her slacks before she quite realized what had happened. He lowered his head to kiss the upper swell of her breasts while he unclasped the demi-cup bra. He caught her fullness lovingly in his hand as the scrap of lacy underwear fell aside.

"Oh!"

Kane's body tautened as Talia's fingers clenched convulsively in his hair, forcing his willing head down a little farther to the tips of her breasts. When he took the nipple of one between his teeth, his hand splaying across her bare stomach, she arched upward, seeking his heat.

"That's it, honey," he grated huskily. "Give yourself to me. I need you so much tonight. I think I'd go out of my head if I didn't solve the rest of the mystery!"

She wanted to ask what he meant, but his fingertips were sliding seductively along the waistband of the slacks, searching for the zipper. Her own hands sought the buttons of his plaid shirt. He murmured something inarticulate as she finished the task of opening the garment.

With a long, satisfied sigh, Talia began creating intimate little paths through the curling red hair. He was irresistble to her tonight, she thought dreamily, and he must have known it. His body lay hard and taut along hers, the bold male bulge beneath his jeans evidence of his desire.

Some part of her knew she shouldn't be this attracted to a man like Kane Sebastian. But another little voice insisted very loudly that even though he came from the world she resented so fiercely, Kane was different. He had said little after dragging the story of scandal out of her, but she had the impression he believed her side of it. And he was helping her find Justin Westbrook. He obviously felt something for her, she told herself, something as strong as what she was feeling for him. She had been told it could happen like this. Love could strike suddenly and without any warning. . . .

It became impossible to think rationally as he slipped off her slacks, leaving Talia in only a tiny triangle of lace below her waist. In the glare of the projector light Kane raised his head to study the length of her body with flaring green eyes.

Slowly he drew his hand from the base of her throat, down across her breasts, and over the gentle curve of her stomach.

"I feel a little drunk," he admitted in a raw, hungry voice. "You're like a drug for me tonight."

The exploring hand swept onward as her glowing amber eyes met his in silent acknowledgment of the sensual tension between them. She wanted him, Talia thought. She wanted him to make passionate love to her and afterward she wanted him to hold her and talk about their future.

When his hand stroked the inner softness of her thigh, her lashes fluttered shut in the ecstatic torment of building desire.

"Please, Kane . . ."

"I will," he promised deeply. "I will."

And then he was beside her, reaching down to lift her into his arms. Through heavy-lidded eyes she absorbed the passion-etched lines of his face as he carried her out of the room, pausing only to shut off the projector.

Into a darkened bedroom he strode, her body curled heavily against him. She felt as if she were floating when he set her down in the center of the huge, shadowy bed.

In the moonlight his green eyes glittered with fire as he unbuckled his belt and stepped out of his jeans.

For a moment he seemed to hesitate by the edge of the bed as if waiting for a sign of her acceptance of him as a lover.

The thought of Kane Sebastian wanting a little reassurance made Talia smile dreamily, feeding the sense of feminine power she had begun to feel over this man the moment he had agreed to her weak attempt at blackmail. She had proven herself as strong as him, held her own with him and now they could come together as equals. As lovers.

Silently she opened her arms and he came into them with a fierce rush of hard, grateful, demanding masculinity.

"Talia! You won't be sorry, sweetheart, I swear it!"

The words came interspersed between a torrent of little scorching kisses. He covered the whole of her body with them, it seemed, compelling her into a twisting, writhing creature of excitement and wonder.

"Kane! Kane, I want you so badly . . ."

She wanted more than that. She wanted to cry out the discovery of her newfound love for him. She wanted to tell him she was his, that she couldn't imagine loving any other man but him now that he had entered her life.

"You're going to have me, sweetheart," he promised a little savagely, "just as I'm going to have you."

He slid down her body, trailing the stinging kisses. Gently he forced apart her legs, his rough thighs moving along her silky ones with undisguised pleasure. The kisses reached her stomach and her hips. And then she was trying to catch her breath as she felt his teeth in the most erotic of caresses on the vulnerable flesh of her inner thigh.

"Please, Kane! Now. I need you now!"

The words were an aching command, but still he held off, his fingers working magic patterns up her legs to the heart of her femininity. Talia didn't think she could take any more. The incredible arousal was going to drive her out of her mind!

"Kane!"

"Darling Talia," he growled against her skin. "Listen to me. Are you protected? Are you . . . are you safe from pregnancy?"

She heard the urgency in him and silently shook her head, wondering how she could have ignored something that crucial. What did this man do to her that she couldn't even think straight?

"No, oh, Kane, no. I'm . . . I'm sorry . . ." How did one explain there were no other lovers currently in one's life? That it had been so long since she had thought herself in love . . . ?

"It's all right, sweetheart," he whispered and she could have sworn there was a thread of satisfaction in his soothing words. "I'll take care of everything."

He pulled away from her for a moment, fumbling with the drawer of the nightstand.

He came back to her a moment later, his body harder and more urgent than ever.

"It's a hell of a temptation not to worry about precautions," he muttered, his fingers fastening themselves in her loosened hair, tearing free what remained of the knot. "Do you realize what I'm saying, Talia?"

She smiled tremulously up at him in the shadowy light, amber eyes almost gold.

"Tonight," he went on, his legs snagging her shifting limbs, "tonight I find there is a side of me that would very badly like to get you pregnant, to chain you to my side . . ."

He lowered his head to her throat. "But I don't have that right. Not yet . . . not yet."

"Kane! Oh, God!"

He covered her body with his own, moving into the ultimate embrace with a fiercely controlled passion that drove her wild with a desire to unleash it.

She almost fought him for the embrace, pulling him to her with an urgency that would have amazed her if she had been able to think about it objectively at that moment. He responded with a sensual power that nearly took away her breath. He was magnificent!

And she told him so with her soft moans, her raking nails, and her arching body.

He gathered her to him, exulting in her reaction to him.

"Talia!" He cried out her name in a voice thick with passion. With a seemingly deliberate attempt to control her shivering, demanding body, he held back the rhythm of the lovemaking, drawing it out until Talia's senses swam.

But slowly her soft pleas and sweetly uninhibited demands seemed to do more to destroy his control than sheer brute force could possibly have done.

Gradually his restraints wore thin and the pace increased to an intoxicating level. Surrendering to the wonder of the moment, Talia wrapped him closer and closer, lifting her body to meet his.

And then, suddenly, everything broke apart around her

in a shimmering, mindless release that enveloped the whole world. She cried out his name, her body shivering ecstatically beneath him.

He followed with an inarticulate moan that was only half muffled against her breast, his body arching rigidly above her for a timeless instant.

Together they clung as the cloud on which they were suspended slowly disintegrated and deposited them onto the soft sheets of the bed.

Talia's eyes fluttered open as she felt Kane roll to one side. His hand trailed lazily across her stomach as she met his still-glowing gaze. She looked up at him lovingly, her mouth soft, her eyes gold, and waited to hear the words she wanted to hear so desperately. Words about a future together.

"Talia, my sweet Talia," he whispered, his head propped on his hand as he gazed down into her love-flushed face.

It might have been the suspicion of humor she thought she saw in those emerald eyes. Or perhaps it was the satisfaction that radiated from him, a satisfaction that seemed more than physical. Whatever the signal, Talia's instincts warned her that the words she was to hear next weren't the ones for which she had longed.

"I brought you here tonight to call your charming bluff," he told her with a hint of an arrogant smile. "Did you guess that?"

The warmth began to seep out of her as she stared up at him in growing confusion. "My bluff?" Her lips were suddenly dry.

"Yes," he said smoothly, "your bluff. Very bad politics, you know, for a man to let a woman start a relationship with a bit of blackmail. What if," he drawled as Talia simply continued to stare, wide-eyed, "what if I told you I've been lying for the past couple of days, sweetheart?"

"Lying! About . . . about what?"

"About sending a cable to South America, of course. What else? What are you going to do, Talia Haywood, would-be blackmailer, now that I'm telling you I never sent that cable? That I don't have any intention of sending it under the circumstances you established. Did you really believe I'd submit so easily to your little blackmail scheme?"

"But, Kane! You said you'd sent it!" She shook her head in a small gesture of restless anxiety. But it wasn't the fact that he'd denied her a lead to Westbrook that was churning her insides and wiping out the warm aftermath of their lovemaking. Just then she didn't care about Westbrook. She only cared about Kane Sebastian and he was telling her he'd tricked her!

"I was only buying a bit of time," he murmured, smiling down at her stricken face. "A bit of time to determine the nature of my tormentor. And now I know the truth. You're not about to go to the papers or anyone else with your tale, are you, sweetheart? Admit it, Talia. Admit you were bluffing all the way!"

She flinched, collecting her chaotic emotions together so that she would have the power to get herself off the bed and away from him.

"Is that why you made love to me, Kane?" she managed through a throat that felt blocked with swallowed tears. "Was it some kind of satisfaction for your male ego to seduce me and then tell me you've been . . . been lying to me? That you never intended to help me?"

Some of the satisfied humor faded from his eyes and the hand on her stomach grew heavy. "I just want to hear you

84

admit the truth. That you couldn't begin to carry out your threats. It isn't in you, is it, Talia? I think I realized it almost from the beginning, but I had to be certain. You're too soft, too gentle for that kind of thing. Damn! When I think of how Hazelton must have had a field day with you . . ."

But Talia had listened to more than enough. She wrenched herself violently to a sitting position, clutching the sheet to her breast. Her love-tangled hair hung in disarray around her shoulders and the amber eyes flashed with a fire that burned her more than the man beside her.

"Damn you, Kane Sebastian," she hissed.

"Admit it, Talia," he ordered, levering himself up beside her, his face hardening. "I want to hear you say the words!"

"All right, I'll give you the words," she flung back, as passionate in her hurt anger as she had been only moments before in her lovemaking. "Why shouldn't I? You've won! You've taught me a lesson, never fear, the lesson I thought I'd learned three years ago from Hazelton. I won't make the mistake of playing with the big boys again. You're all alike, aren't you? I knew that when I walked into your office. But you're cleverer than Hazelton; I'll give you that much credit. You really had me fooled. Of course I wouldn't dream of going to the papers with my tale. I never intended to carry out my threats in the first place. You're absolutely right, I don't have the guts for genuine blackmail. It would have been a little kinder of you to call my bluff before the big seduction scene, though. But only a fool would expect kindness from men like you and Hazelton."

"Talia! Calm down and listen to me, you little wildcat," he commanded with an astonishingly soothing tone. What did he think he was doing now? "It's over. You tried your silly game and I called your bluff. We're even. Honey, I couldn't let you get away with thinking you'd blackmailed me into helping you."

"I didn't think that!" she cried. "At least not after the first meeting in your office! By the time we'd finished dinner that night I got the impression you were helping me because you wanted to help me! And don't you dare talk about us being even. We're not even! You just won the victory and you know it!"

She began edging backward off the rumpled bed, trying to hold the sheet against her with one hand and tugging it free of the mattress in the process. With a swift, striking movement, Kane reached out and grabbed her wrist with the manacle of his fingers.

"Simmer down," he murmured in a throaty growl. "Stop raging at me. You deserved to be shown up for that stupid blackmail attempt and you know it. But it's over. I'm satisfied and you've admitted that kind of game isn't exactly your style. I haven't said I *won't* help you; I've only said I won't do it under the influence of blackmail."

"You've made your point!" She struggled to free her hand, but he wouldn't release the captive wrist. The flags of anger and humiliation flew high in her cheeks. At least there had been no awful bedroom scene with Derek Hazelton! She wouldn't have gone to bed with that man for the world. But she'd tumbled so easily into Kane Sebastian's velvet trap!

"If I've made my point," he told her in a gentling tone, "then come back to bed and try other tactics. I can be persuaded, you know," he added with a suggestive smile. "But I prefer that you use some other means than blackmail—"

86

He never finished the sentence. Talia dropped the sheet, swinging her hand in a fierce arc that ended with a cracking sound against his cheek.

It was no ladylike slap. It carried the full force of her anger and bitterness behind it and the blow shocked Kane into releasing her wrist. The hand he had been using to chain her went to his reddening cheek in astonishment as he stared up at Talia.

"The price of doing business with you, Kane? Having an affair? Forget it. I won't pay that particular price. Ask Derek Hazelton!"

She was on her feet now, proudly naked beside the bed. Before he could respond, she swung around on her heel and strode from the room, her chin high.

"Talia! Where the hell do you think you're going?"

He was scrambling to his feet behind her. Talia didn't look back. She walked into the bath, turned on the shower, and stepped under it. The bathroom door opened as the hot water steamed around her.

"What do you think you're doing?" he shouted above the roar of the water.

"What does it look like? I'm trying to get clean. I feel a little dirty!"

A long moment passed during which Talia scrubbed violently at her skin. She was almost through when the shower stall door opened and Kane stepped in beside her, his face set. The green eyes were chips of emerald ice as he confronted her.

"At the rate you're going," he warned very softly, "it won't be long before I lose my temper."

Talia ignored the leashed fury in him, finishing her rinsing while stubbornly refusing to meet his eyes. Deliberately she turned away from the sight of the powerful male body so close to hers. To think that only a few moments ago she had willingly lost herself in his arms, held that body to her with love and an unbelievable passion. And all along he was only playing with her. Punishing her.

When she attempted to force her way past him, he caught her around the waist, hugging her back against his hip.

"Talia, listen to me : . ."

"Please don't say anything more," she begged, not fighting him but standing slackly in his hold.

"You're overreacting and you know it! You deserved being strung along for a while"

"I deserved it," she agreed with alacrity. "And, yes, I'm definitely overreacting." She stared stonily at the shower door, willing him to relax his grip. She could feel the strong male thigh against her rounded bottom and the intimacy of his grasp made her overwhelmingly aware of the physical effect he had on her. What was wrong with her to be so easily seduced by this man? How could she have thought herself in love with him?

He waited suspiciously, obviously expecting further argument on her part. When none came he squeezed her gently and then let her go.

"All right," he said slowly as she stepped out of the shower and reached for a towel. "I'll be out in a minute. I'll make some coffee and we can talk."

Talia barely heard the last word. She was already on her way out of the bathroom, seeking her scattered clothes.

By the time the water had been turned off in the shower she was dressed and headed for the front door. Kane spotted her as she made her way past him down the hall, her eyes focused straight ahead.

"Talia, come back here. You're not going anywhere and you know it. What do you think you're going to do? Find a cab cruising out here miles from town?"

She opened the front door and closed it firmly behind her even as he was reaching frantically for his jeans. She walked past the Lotus and found the main street which wound down to the guard gate. There would be someone on duty down there, she decided grimly, someone who might be willing to help her.

She heard the front door open and slam shut with a savage sound as she walked briskly down the road. Her tousled hair shone in a halo around her head beneath the glow of the streetlamps. Behind her the Lotus roared to life.

"Get in, you stubborn little witch," Kane ordered as he slowed the car beside her. She could feel the raging, frustrated anger in him.

For the first time, she turned to face him, coming to a halt on the sidewalk.

"No, thanks," she said finally, reading the male intent in his face. "I'll walk."

"Talia, don't be a fool. Get in and I'll take you back to your hotel if that's really what you want!" he exploded, leaning across to push open the passenger door.

She considered him carefully in the streetlight and decided he might be telling the truth. "If you don't take me back to the hotel, I'll start screaming so loudly your neighbors will call the guard at the gate," she finally stated.

"More threats?" he murmured laconically, waiting.

"I mean every word this time, Kane."

He held her eyes for a long moment. "I believe you." He sighed in disgust. "Get in."

Without a word, Talia slid into the front seat of the

Lotus and without a word, Kane took a savage grip on the wheel and headed the car back toward Sacramento.

The only words that were spoken were finally said by Kane as he broodingly searched her cold, composed face at the hotel door.

"I'll stop by before work in the morning. We'll have a cup of coffee and we'll talk. Do you understand?"

Talia nodded mutely. She didn't care. She would be long gone by then.

CHAPTER FIVE

It was nearly noon three days later when Karen Thornton, receptionist, secretary, and general handyperson of Advanced Management Designs stuck her head around Talia's door.

"Sorry to interrupt," she said with a quick smile for the distinguished, middle-aged man sitting across the desk from Talia, "but there's someone to see you, Talia."

"A student?" Talia frowned slightly, glancing up from the sales figures she was going over with Harold Grayson, her boss. Harold was the owner of Advanced Management Designs and in him Talia had at last found a boss who practiced what he firmly believed in—sound, ethical management. Talia had always privately thought the reason he did so was that he could afford to. A.M.D. was a small operation, composed chiefly of the teaching staff plus Karen and Harold. There were no significant managerial positions or vice-presidencies to which Talia and the other instructors could aspire, so there was a minimum of power-maneuvering behind the scenes. Harold could easily play the role of respected leader.

"No, he's not a student. Won't give a name, but I don't think it's a personal matter. The guy looks"—Karen hesitated, narrowing her attractive blue-eyed gaze thoughtfully—"a little too businesslike, if you know what I mean."

"Go ahead and see him, Talia," Harold directed graciously, inclining his silver head and forcing his portly figure to his feet. "I was on my way to lunch anyway. We can go over these figures this afternoon."

Harold smiled at the pretty, blond secretary on his way out. He was always on time for lunch. Karen smiled back automatically and then turned to Talia. "Shall I show him in?"

"Go ahead." Talia nodded, collecting the charts and graphs she'd been studying and placing them into a neat pile. Automatically she reached for her coffee cup. She was so tired today. But, then, she had been feeling tired and listless since the long drive back to San Jose three days ago. No amount of attention to her work could dull the ache in her heart or wipe out the memory of her foolishness.

She sipped her coffee by the window, waiting for Karen to show her visitor into the office. Talia had never been overly fond of San Jose. One of the nation's fastest-growing cities, it spread out from the southern tip of San Francisco Bay in a sprawl of subdivisions and industrial parks.

That last night in Sacramento . . . . Talia took another sip of coffee and shut her eyes on the memory. What a fool she had been. How could she possibly have thought that what she felt for Kane Sebastian had been the stirrings of love. In the three days they'd known each other? Never had a man affected her so quickly, aroused her passions so easily. She flinched from the thought of how completely she had surrendered. She would give anything to be able to call back that night in his arms.

"Your visitor, Miss Haywood," Karen announced formally from the doorway, a tinge of disapproval in her voice. Karen didn't appreciate clients who refused to be properly introduced.

Talia swung around, a polite smile on her lips, to find a man of medium height in his early forties standing beside Karen. He was conservatively dressed in a suit that did not quite successfully hide a small paunch. Receding sandy hair was neatly combed and cut very short. Brown eyes met hers in a cool, distantly polite glance. The face was attractive enough, Talia thought, if one didn't mind that hint of weakness in the chin and eyes.

"Can I help you?" she asked calmly, almost glad of any excuse not to have to think of the time in Sacramento. She walked forward to stand behind her desk and indicated the chair across from her.

The sandy-haired man nodded once and pulled a leather folder out of his jacket as Karen closed the door behind him.

"Aaron Pomeroy, Miss Haywood. Federal Bureau of Investigation."

He snapped open the leather wallet, giving Talia a brief glimpse of a badge and an identity card which she was too stunned to read. She barely had time to notice that the picture on the card vaguely matched the man standing across from her.

"FBI!" she echoed as Pomeroy pocketed the identification. "What in the world do you want with me?" She sank down onto her chair and Aaron Pomeroy politely took his

93

seat. He smiled with a professional reassurance that for some reason irritated Talia.

"I'm here to ask you a few questions about a man named Justin Gage Westbrook, Miss Haywood," he explained easily.

Talia stared at him, some part of her mind registering the fact that Aaron Pomeroy's smile definitely did not reach his brown eyes. They remained very cool, very direct. In fact, she thought grimly, they were almost like marbles. She shivered. What had she done?

"I'm sorry, Mr. Pomeroy, you've taken me by surprise. What in the world could the FBI want with me or Mr. Westbrook?" Deliberately Talia made a bid to steady herself. Some very basic warning bells were sounding. Bells she'd never heard before but which came alive instinctively. Perhaps that's what unexpected calls from FBI agents did to one. She felt her mind switch into a surprisingly careful, surprisingly fast gear. Mentally she ran through a list of lawyers, which was absolutely ridiculous. She'd certainly done nothing illegal.

"There's nothing to be alarmed about, Miss Haywood," Pomeroy told her in a falsely soothing tone that annoyed Talia even more. It was as if he had assessed the degree of his impact on her and was satisfied. Why did every male on earth think she could be easily intimidated? Damn it! Part of her taxes went to pay this man's salary. He worked for her.

"I'm relieved to hear that," she managed to retort coolly.

"But we would like to ask you a few questions," he persisted. "It has come to our attention that you've been inquiring into the career of Mr. Westbrook, seeking information on him even though according to our information, you've already been informed of his death in Africa. Correct?"

What was this all about? To her knowledge, Westbrook had never worked for the FBI. Justin's profession had always taken him to other parts of the globe and everyone knew the FBI was limited to domestic matters.

"I have made a few inquiries about him," she admitted slowly. "It's been something of a hobby. He was a friend of my father's, you see. We . . . that is, my family and I, always wondered what had become of him."

She found herself regulating the words, striving for a casual, polite calm. In her lap Talia's palms grew moist and she prayed such things couldn't be detected by men like this.

"You were aware of his reported death a few years ago?"

"Yes."

"Yet you recently began inquiring into one of the assignments he carried out within a year of his death. An assignment he undertook in South America. May I ask why, Miss Haywood?"

Talia watched him narrowly. She didn't like the man. There was something about him that made her distrustful. Weren't FBI agents supposed to come across as competent, patriotic, and trustworthy?

"Curiosity, Mr. Pomeroy," she stated as matter-of-factly as possible. "I was simply trying to trace Westbrook's career up until the time of his death. A puzzle, if you like."

"I see."

He waited, but Talia refused to be stampeded into volunteering more information than was absolutely necessary. An elemental management technique, she reminded herself determinedly. Never take the risk of volunteering too much. She forced a bland smile and did a little waiting herself.

Pomeroy cleared his throat and forged ahead. Talia suddenly felt as if she were in a room with a slightly overweight snake. "The Bureau would be interested in knowing, Miss Haywood, if you, personally, have any reason to believe Justin Westbrook is still alive. If that, in fact, is your reason for your recent inquiries."

Well, that was easy enough to answer. "No reason whatsoever, Mr. Pomeroy. I have absolutely no indication that he's still alive." *Nothing but my own intuition,* she added silently, *which I'm not about to share with the FBI. At least, not this particular representative of it!*

"Then why, may I ask, did you go all the way up to Sacramento in person a few days ago to interview the president of the company for whom Westbrook worked while in South America?"

He sat back with grim anticipation, clearly certain he'd dropped a bombshell on her.

"It's not that far, Mr. Pomeroy," she returned mildly, the alarm bells growing louder in her head. How did Pomeroy know of that trip? Good God! Was the FBI following her? "I simply drove up to meet with the head of the company because I thought he might have some personal knowledge of Mr. Westbrook which would be interesting. He didn't."

"Then why, Miss Haywood," Pomeroy shot back as if closing a trap, "did you wind up spending three days in Sacramento?"

Quite suddenly more than caution began guiding Talia's response now. She found herself thinking in terms of survival. Not her own—Justin Westbrook's. What if he *were* still alive? What had she done to him by creating this trail?

For the first time she considered just what implications might be involved if Westbrook were, indeed, alive. The gnawing problem of loyalty surfaced.

Westbrook had been her father's closest friend during the Korean war and afterward for several years. She knew they had saved each other's lives. And even though contact had diminished to nothing between them over the years there was never any doubt in Talia's mind that a special relationship had always existed between her father and Justin Westbrook.

And now the FBI was asking her questions. It occurred to Talia that if the Federal Bureau of Investigation couldn't find Justin, it might very well be because he wanted it that way. And the only logical reason for Pomeroy's presence in her office today was because the FBI or *someone* didn't believe Westbrook was dead.

She resisted the impulse to lick her dry lips. In a strange way she had inherited the mantle of friendship Justin had shared with her father. She couldn't explain it, but she felt a responsibility toward the fascinating, little-known figure from her childhood. And she felt a responsibility toward her dead father.

Talia forced a smile, but the warm color that crept into her cheekbones didn't need forcing. It came naturally. Talk about social lies!

"Mr. Pomeroy, I've told you the truth about Energy Interface Systems not being able to help me. They knew little or nothing about Justin Westbrook. However, Mr. Sebastian and I—" She broke off delicately.

"Yes, Miss Haywood?" Pomeroy pressed, eyes narrowing.

"Mr. Sebastian and I got along rather well together," she concluded weakly, lowering her eyes with what she

97

hoped was a properly demure, possibly slightly embarrassed expression. "He invited me out to dinner and I accepted. One thing led to another and . . ." She waved a hand in graceful dismissal of the rest of the sentence.

"You're telling me that your reasons for staying the three days in Sacramento were personal? Not related to information Energy Interface Systems was digging up for you?" Pomeroy bit out coldly.

"I'm afraid so. I was told from the very beginning that they really couldn't help me in regard to Westbrook."

"Miss Haywood, I'll be frank with you. If you have any indication at all that Justin Westbrook might still be alive, we want to know about it. The information could be crucial." Pomeroy appeared to hesitate and then come to a decision. "There is some indication, you see, that in his last years, Westbrook might have been acting against the best interests of his country."

And that, for some reason, helped Talia make her own decision. Justin Westbrook a traitor? It was inconceivable. Men like her father and Justin Westbrook did not turn against their country. She knew that in the depths of her bones. She would not help Aaron Pomeroy.

"I don't know what information you think I might be able to obtain that would not already have come into your own hands, Mr. Pomeroy. Surely the resources at your command are far superior to my own. In any event, I can assure you that as far as I'm concerned, Westbrook is dead. I've only been trying to fill in the story of his rather unusual career for the sake of family interest. I never dreamed that there might be any questions to ask beyond the time of his death in Africa."

"And you're quite certain the time you spent in Sacramento was strictly because of your, er, growing interest in Kane Sebastian?"

Why did he harp on that? "I assure you, Mr. Pomeroy," she said calmly with a charming smile that took a tremendous effort, "I would never have spent most of the night with Kane Sebastian at his place if I had been intent only on discussing Justin Westbrook!"

"Spent the night? Oh, I see . . ." He cleared his throat again. "You're telling me you and Sebastian became involved in only a few days?"

"It happens that way sometimes," Talia said, keeping all traces of bitterness out of her voice with an effort of will. Her smile broadened deliberately. "Come now, Mr. Pomeroy, doesn't the FBI believe in love at first sight?" She could hardly believe her own words.

"You will be seeing Sebastian again?" Pomeroy didn't appear amused.

"I certainly hope so," she smiled coyly.

"The Bureau has absolutely no interest in your personal relationships. But we would very much like to be kept informed if you should ever learn anything that might indicate Westbrook didn't die in Africa. Do I make myself quite clear, Miss Haywood?"

"Very."

"Here's a number where I can be reached."

She watched him scrawl the phone number on a slip of paper and place it on her desk. Politely she reached across and retrieved it. "I'll certainly let you know if I ever turn up anything," she lied, "but, frankly, I think my search is over. It would have been nice to fill in the few little gaps about his career in South America, but that doesn't appear to be possible. And I certainly don't want to go any further

99

and find out an old family friend might have turned traitor!"

The marble eyes narrowed. "I can understand that. But the FBI relies heavily on citizen cooperation in its work, so please call that number if anything comes up or if you remember anything you think would be helpful."

"I understand, but, as I said, I think I've reached the point where I'll be calling a halt to my little hobby," Talia said smoothly as she saw him to the door. "Besides," she murmured with a meaningful smile, "I seem to have developed other interests lately."

Aaron Pomeroy shot her a cold glance. God! Brown eyes should be warm, not chips of dark marble, Talia thought uncomfortably. "Sebastian?"

She nodded, opening the door for him. "Perhaps I owe Westbrook something for the introduction?" She chuckled.

Perhaps it was an inevitable fate that she had tempted too often during the past few moments that placed Kane Sebastian in the outer office precisely at the moment Talia was escorting Aaron Pomeroy of out Advanced Management Designs.

Perhaps it was simply the streak of bad luck she seemed to be having lately.

Whatever the reason, it was very nearly Talia's undoing. She was already suffering a bad case of nerves, but it seemed as if some vicious deity was intent on pushing her over the edge altogether.

He was standing in front of Karen's desk, his craggy face intent and serious as he talked quietly to the secretary. The snug-fitting jeans and open-necked shirt brought back violent memories of three days ago. As if, Talia thought wretchedly, she needed any more memories.

What was he doing here? Had he come to torment her further?

There was no time to scream at him, no time to demand explanations, no time to slam the door in his face. Aaron Pomeroy had also seen the tall, lean man standing in the lobby and by the narrowing of the brown marble gaze, Talia knew he'd recognized him.

At that moment Kane glanced up, green eyes pinning Talia's stunned face with unerring accuracy. He ignored the watchful man by her side entirely and started forward. There was an almost frightening determination in the gliding stride that brought him toward her.

In that painful moment one salient fact seemed blazingly clear to Talia. She had given Aaron Pomeroy the idea that she had started an affair with Kane Sebastian. Something warned her she'd better make certain the notion stuck.

"Kane! You made it! How delightful. I was so afraid we would have to wait until next weekend!"

Pulling every ounce of acting ability she'd ever owned to the fore, Talia left Pomeroy's side to greet Kane with the charmingly expectant smile of a woman confident of her reception.

Hands extended to take his, she stood on tiptoe for his kiss, lifting her mouth with an inviting smile. To her amazement, the smile stayed in place even as his fingers wrapped around hers and crushed them with an urgent grip the strength of which she didn't think Kane was even aware of.

"Hello, honey," he growled and then delivered the fleeting kiss of welcome Talia was so clearly expecting. Only she was aware of the fierce hardness of his mouth on hers and the hold that was chasing all the blood out of her fingers. The green eyes were emerald fires as she stepped back.

"Kane, darling, I want you to meet someone. A Mr. Pomeroy . . ."

Talia turned, intent on the introduction, just as the outer door closed on her recent visitor. She stared in astonishment at the closed door and then became conscious of the painful grip on her hand.

Slowly she turned back to Kane, deliberately trying to loosen her fingers. She got one hand free, but he refused to release the other.

"Sorry I missed meeting your visitor, honey," he drawled, "but why don't you carry on with the introductions? I was just on the point of letting this young woman know who I am."

He waited, daring her to change her approach now. Talia could sense the challenge in him. She had started this and he was intent on making her finish.

"Of course," she agreed, refusing to let him intimidate her. Hadn't she just faced down an agent of the Federal Bureau of Investigation? "Karen, this is Kane Sebastian, a . . . friend of mine."

"How do you do, Mr. Sebastian." Karen nodded eagerly, blue eyes clearly approving. "As you can see," she added with a light laugh, "Miss Haywood is free now. Go on in!"

"Thanks." Kane tossed her an engaging grin and turned expectantly toward Talia.

There really was no option, Talia thought sadly. Head high, the smile still firmly in place, she led the way into her office.

As soon as he had stepped past her, she closed the door with the tiniest of slams and leaned back against it, eyeing him vengefully as he swept the small, plain office with a curious gaze.

"All right, Kane. What do you want?"

He walked over to her window and peered out. There was no sweeping panorama as he enjoyed from his high-rise building. A.M.D. occupied a second floor suite of offices and classrooms.

"I came to see you, naturally." He glanced back over his shoulder laconically. "And I got the strange impression you were glad to see me."

Talia braced herself, both hands behind her on the door-knob, and met his gaze. "You walked in at an inopportune moment," she told him flatly. "Not that any one moment would have been more opportune than the next."

"You're so good for my ego."

"I've fed your ego all I intend to give it," she shot back furiously.

"So why the little welcome scene out there in the lob-by?"

"That man who was with me . . ."

"An ex-lover?" The question was as subtle as a stiletto, Talia thought.

"Not quite. He's an FBI agent. Or so he says."

"What?"

That got his full attention. He swung around and reached for the chair Pomeroy had recently occupied, throwing himself into it with a lithe grace that made Talia think of other things. The green eyes slitted. "Let's hear it. Everything."

"Nobody's contacted you?" she asked warily, releasing her death grip on the door handle to make her way across the room to her own chair.

"No. Certainly not the FBI!"

"He wants to know why I'm asking questions about Justin. He wants to know if I think he may still be alive and he warned me that Justin might have . . . have turned traitor," she told Kane evenly, not looking at him. She kept her gaze on the building across the street, the tension in her body almost unbearable. It was really too much. Dealing with the FBI was bad enough, but to have to cope with Kane Sebastian on top of it seemed the height of unfairness. But, as her father had once said, nobody had promised any degree of fairness in the world.

"And what," Kane asked coolly, "did you tell Pomeroy?"

Talia bit her lip, her hands clasped together in her lap. "I lied to him, Kane." Her voice was barely audible. "I sat here in this chair and lied to an agent of the Federal Bureau of Investigation. I told him I believed Justin Westbrook is dead and then I fed him a few . . . a few choice lines about my relationship with you."

"You told him we were lovers?" he asked laconically.

Talia almost winced at the strangely neutral tone of his voice. She nodded once, her sleek head moving in a regal motion. "I told him you could give me absolutely no information on Justin Westbrook and that after our initial interview, our relationship had continued on a strictly personal basis. When you showed up out there in the lobby just as he was leaving, I couldn't think of anything else to do except make the story look real."

There was a pause that lasted so long, Talia finally had to look at him. Kane was watching her with an enigmatic gaze that was far more unnerving than Aaron Pomeroy's marble stare. This gaze did more than cause her palms to dampen in nervousness. Kane Sebastian had a way of sending shivers down her spine.

"Don't look so frightened," he drawled, lounging back in his chair, booted feet stretched out in front of him. "You told the man the truth. We are lovers."

Talia flung up her head proudly. "Hardly," she snapped. "A one-night-stand brought about through a willful deceit on your part doesn't give us the status of lovers!"

He shook his head, a low whistle coming from between his teeth. "I don't know how you do it, but you have a way of making me feel guilty. I have to keep reminding myself that I'm the innocent party in all this. You were trying to blackmail me."

"If you've come here to continue haranguing me about that, forget it. You've had all the revenge you're going to get."

He ignored that. "Why did you run away, Talia? I told you we would talk about it."

"There wasn't anything left to talk about that I could see. Now please tell me what you're doing here, Kane. I've got a lot on my mind today and I don't intend to listen to your macho gloating!"

"I come bearing gifts in a disgustingly unmacho attempt to bribe my way back into your affections," he grated icily.

Talia waited warily, every fiber of her being alive to his presence. How long would it be before she could forget that night? How long before she no longer remembered her response in this man's arms?

"You don't trust me, do you?" he murmured almost idly.

"The feeling is mutual, I'm sure."

He sucked in his breath in an audible sound of annoyance. "Aren't you even interested in my gift?"

105

"Not particularly." Damned if she would accept anything from him!

"Not even if I'm bringing you the gift of a possible clue to the whereabouts of Justin Westbrook?"

CHAPTER SIX

Talia stared at him in stunned amazement. "You sent the cable?"

"The morning you ran away," he admitted, sounding quite disgusted with himself. "I was going to do it all along. I just didn't want you to think you were getting my help through blackmail. But when I arrived that morning to find out you'd skipped town, I realized it was going to take a major peace bribe to soothe your ruffled feathers."

"You expect me to sleep with you for the information?" she whispered tautly.

"Coming back into my bed would be a very nice gesture of gratitude on your part, of course," he began almost wistfully. But when she glared at him, eyes burning gold, he lifted a hand placatingly and his mouth twisted in a little smile of surrender. "Don't worry, the information is yours without any major strings attached."

"I . . . I don't know what to say, Kane." Talia tried desperately to analyze the situation the way she taught her students. This was a scene loaded with power dynamics, and as far as she could see, Kane held all the leverage. Why should he walk in here and give her something for nothing? Men like Kane Sebastian were seldom altruistic! Did he really expect her to sleep with him out of gratitude for the information? After what he'd done to her?

"I do have one small request . . ." he murmured delicately.

"I knew it!"

"I would like a full explanation of your friend Pomeroy. Is that too much to ask? Things seem to have gotten a little more complicated since we last talked," he concluded dryly.

Talia considered that. She badly wanted to talk to someone and Kane knew more of the story now than anyone else, in addition to which, in spite of her personal hostility toward him, she realized she trusted him in some strange fashion. He wouldn't deliberately jeopardize Justin Westbrook's safety any more than she would. And it would be such a relief to discuss this with a logical man like Kane.

"Pomeroy scared me, Kane," Talia finally said flatly.

The green eyes narrowed. Quite suddenly all the wistfulness and the placating qualities vanished from his expression.

"Did he threaten you?"

She shook her head quickly, not liking the hardness in him. "No, no, it wasn't that. It was just that he made me realize what I might be doing to Westbrook, what I might already have done. If . . . if Justin's still alive, there's probably a very good reason why he doesn't want to be found. I may have created a path that will lead straight to him. A path someone like Pomeroy can follow. There's

108

something strange about Pomeroy, Kane. And that scares me too."

"Go on."

"Well, why would the FBI start asking questions? Justin didn't work for them. He was often attached to various agencies, but he always worked overseas, never in this country, to my knowledge. The FBI is limited to domestic matters, I believe. And why would Pomeroy ask me questions but not you? He wants to know what I found out about the South American assignment, but he didn't talk to you. Theoretically you could have told him more on that subject. Yet when you appeared on my doorstep a few minutes ago, he practically fled. Why?"

There was a distinct pause. "Because he's not really from the FBI?"

The suspicion voiced at last, Talia breathed a small sigh of relief. "It would explain a lot. It would also make me feel a great deal better!"

"Worried about having lied to a genuine agent?"

"Yes," she admitted starkly.

"Don't fret," he murmured. "If Pomeroy turns out to be the real thing, I'll gladly perjure myself on your behalf."

"For a price?" The words were out before she could stop them.

"Only if you want to pay it," he snapped back coolly.

"Kane, this is ridiculous. Tell me why you're here. The real reason. I don't need any more mysteries in my life at the moment!"

"I want you," he answered simply.

"You've had me," she flung at him, goaded. "And, believe me, I felt *had*!"

To Talia's amazement, he turned a dull red despite his tan.

"Like I said," he muttered laconically, "I have to keep reminding myself that it was you who were blackmailing me!"

He surged to his feet, one hand raking roughly through the thick chestnut hair, and paced to the window. "Can't we agree to give each other another chance, Talia?"

"Why?" she whispered, her eyes riveted to his back.

He seemed to deliberate over his answer. Staring out the window, he finally suggested softly, "How about for the sake of what we had that night?"

"For the sake of one night in bed? You've got to be joking! That was a power trip you were on that night. You made that very clear afterward. It was nothing more meaningful than a means of satisfying your ego by getting back at me. How about if I admit I deserved it? Will that be enough to make you leave me alone?" she blazed.

"No, damn it!"

With three incredibly swift, gliding steps he was beside her, reaching down to pull her roughly to her feet and into his arms.

"You're the only thing that can satisfy me," he rasped just before his mouth came down on hers with the impact of an invading army.

Clamped to his taut, urgent strength with fingers of steel that circled her upper arms, Talia stood helplessly still beneath the onslaught. Her mouth was forced open beneath the frustrated male anger in his kiss.

Desperately she tried to defend the soft, warm territory behind her lips, using her teeth furiously on the tip of his tongue. But he returned the small punishment with calculated warning, catching her lower lip between his own teeth.

Talia gasped at the threat and instinctively halted her poor defense. Seizing the initiative once more, Kane forced her closer, releasing her arms to gather her more fully into the embrace. She felt the hard edge of his belt buckle digging into her flesh through the fabric of her white skirt and for some obscure reason the discomfort whetted her anger.

As his mouth slid moistly on hers, forcing her to admit its dominance, Talia kicked wildly at his leg, seeking any target within range.

Kane swore violently as her blow landed, but he didn't release her. He lifted his head, green eyes flaming.

"You've got a hell of a lot of nerve, woman, do you know that? You walk into my life and threaten me with blackmail. When I call you on it, you run off in a move calculated to make me feel guilty. When I come after you, offering the only gift I have to offer as a bribe for your forgiveness, you treat me as if you can barely stand the sight of me!"

"Feeling put upon, Kane?" she hissed tauntingly.

"Damn right I'm feeling put upon! And just this once I'm going to make you do the apologizing!"

"Kane!"

Her startled exclamation came too late. He had lowered himself into her leather swivel chair, pulling her down into his lap and pinning her securely against him.

"All I'm asking for is one kiss, freely given," he growled. "A kiss like the ones I had from you that night . . ."

Before she could say anything more, he was taking her mouth once more. But even though he held her tightly,

111

preventing any struggle, the kiss itself was no longer filled with his frustration and anger. Instead it was deliberately seductive, coaxing, even pleading.

And it brought back all the warm, soft memories of that night she had spent in his arms. The memories she had been trying so hard to block out of her mind. Talia's lashes fluttered shut in an effort to banish him from her senses, to seal herself off from the closeness of him, the intoxicating male scent of his body, the well-remembered strength in the hands now holding her so firmly.

It was hopeless. This time when his tongue slid, searching, between her lips, it was with a nerve-tingling sensuality that stirred the embers he had left smoldering. With the unexplained suddenness of the longing that had come upon her that night, Talia found herself wanting him once more.

She heard the soft moan in her own throat and knew, as Kane surely must, that it signaled the beginning of her surrender.

"Please, Talia," he grated huskily. "Please agree to give us both a second chance."

He withdrew from her mouth a fraction of an inch, meeting her eyes as she looked up at him through her lashes. The hand pinning hers to her side lifted to stroke back the tendrils of hair that had come loose from the gold clip she wore.

"Why?" she managed breathlessly.

"Why? My God, Talia!" he groaned. "Can't you see why? Do you think I routinely chase after lady blackmailers who make a practice of lying to Federal agents?"

"Kane!"

"I'm sorry, honey." He soothed her at once, his face

112

softening as he stroked the line of her cheek with curious fingers. "I'm only teasing you . . ."

"No, you're not," she sighed. "It's the truth. All of it."

"And I'm no better than you," he agreed, a slow grin appearing. "I tricked you into thinking I was going to play victim and then turned the tables on you. When you ran off, I immediately sent the cable, and went crazy waiting for an answer so I'd have bargaining material, and then I came after you on my hands and knees."

"Your hands and knees!" she squeaked, thunderstruck with the ludicrous exaggeration.

"Well, almost," he temporized.

"Almost, nothing! You were hoping to talk me back into bed in exchange for that information, and you know it!"

"I'll admit I had my hopes, but I'm not going to force the issue," he defended righteously. "I'll settle for starting over."

"Starting what over?" she asked suspiciously, melting in spite of herself. She knew she shouldn't allow him to manipulate her this way, but something in him was reaching out to her. She had thought herself falling in love with Kane that night at his condominium. It was irrational, but all that happened afterward didn't seem able to destroy the memories or kill the fires he had ignited. A part of her wanted to respond to him.

"Our relationship."

"Did we have one?" she forced herself to demand mockingly.

He lifted one red brow and very deliberately moved his hand to the curve of her breast. When she sucked in her breath, staring silently up at him, he nodded slowly.

"Yes, we have one. It's a little rocky at the moment and

113

it got off to a bad start, but it exists and I want to give it another chance. You intrigue me and attract me and make me want to protect you when I'm mad enough to want to wring that lovely neck. I find myself willing to lie to poor Pomeroy on your behalf and willing to hand over my one bargaining tool without any assurance that it will convince you to take pity on me."

"You'll tell me where Justin Westbrook is?" she whispered, searching his intent face as she listened to him. She had the distinct impression he was telling the truth. He wanted her. And she could hardly go on denying to herself that she wanted him.

"I'll do better than that. I'll take you to him. Or, at least, I'll take you to where my information says he might be. I can't make any guarantees, honey. Westbrook may have left another false trail. It could all be another dead end for you," he added as if compelled to lay all the cards on the table.

"I realize that," she said slowly.

"What about it?" He half-smiled, only the rasping quality of his voice betraying the intensity of his emotion. "Shall we call a truce and start over?"

Talia lay quiescently in his arms, forcing herself to consider the ramifications of what he was suggesting. She was so tempted, so very tempted. But this time, she promised herself, she would force a slower pace. This time they would go slowly with each other, find out for certain if what they had was real.

For the first time since she had fled Sacramento, Talia felt a wisp of humor come to life.

"Are you quite certain," she asked in liquid tones, "that you want to be associated with me?

The green eyes flared with an answering gleam. "I'll

114

take my chances. Do we have a deal? My information for your agreement to start over?"

"I thought," she mused from her dangerous position in his lap, "that you were prepared to hand over the information without any assurances . . ."

"Talia! Don't tease me. Not now!"

"All right, Kane," she said quickly and soothingly as she felt the renewed tension in his hold. "I'll agree to . . . to explore the possibilities of a relationship. But I'm not agreeing to jump back into bed with you," she added hastily as she sensed the leap of satisfaction in him.

Carefully he stood and set her back on her feet. "We'll discuss that aspect of the situation later," he drawled, bending to brush her lips with his own. "Over dinner."

"Dinner?"

"That's when I hand over my information, naturally. And that's when we should also have a serious discussion about what to do with your Mr. Pomeroy."

Yes, Talia thought uneasily. She badly wanted to talk about that. Who was Aaron Pomeroy and was he a threat to Justin? To her? It would be good to share her worries and thoughts with Kane, she realized, no longer questioning her strange trust in him. It was there. She'd just have to accept it as a fact of life.

"Don't you have to go back to Sacramento?" She smiled uncertainly.

"I've arranged to take a few days off."

"A few days!"

"Umm," he confirmed smoothly. "Long enough for us to track down Justin Westbrook. Something tells me I'm not going to have any peace at all until that mystery is solved."

"Where . . . where are you staying?"

"You mean I'm not getting an invitation to stay at your place?" he quipped, managing to look reproachful and hurt. When he caught the sizzling gold gaze in return, he held up a hand. "Okay, okay. I'll stay in a nearby motel. Any suggestions?"

She thought a moment and gave him one. "Oh, and you'll need my address," she went on unthinkingly.

"I've already got that," he grinned from the door. "How do you think I found you today? It was on all those nice notes you wrote to my Personnel Department."

He was gone before Talia could think of a response, leaving her to the grim realization that, thanks to all her unannounced visitors, she wasn't going to get any lunch.

Well, it would leave her with a healthy appetite for dinner, she told herself bracingly as she picked up a notebook and headed for the afternoon seminar she was giving for a local company's up-and-coming group of managers.

Hours later, as she dressed for dinner, she didn't hesitate long at the closet. It would have to be the knee-length, soft, black sheath with its glitter of gold zig-zag trim at cuffs and hem. There was something about a black dress, Talia decided as she slipped into the garment, that gave a woman a feeling of being in control of an evening. Dark stockings and low-heeled black shoes with gold-rimmed black satin flowers completed the allover look of cool sophistication.

She wrapped her tawny hair into an elegant topknot, allowing wispy tendrils to trail invitingly down a neck bared by the low, curving neckline of the dress. When the doorbell chimed, she went to answer it, scooping up the Chinese-print, gold silk shawl she'd set out earlier and letting it flow over one arm.

"No cowboy boots?" she drawled as she took in the

116

sight of Kane in a sleek, European-cut suit that emphasized his look of coiled, lean strength.

He glanced down at the polished Italian leather shoes he was wearing. "I should have thought about that, shouldn't I? Would have been good protection in the event you decide to take another cheap shot like you did today in your office."

"I couldn't have done much damage," she retorted spiritedly, hiding a wince as she remembered the kick she'd aimed at him earlier. "You barely even flinched at the time, as I recall!"

"A man's not supposed to flinch," he reminded her dryly. "Ready?"

She nodded, a sense of excitement gripping her that had absolutely nothing to do with the information on Justin Westbrook that Kane had promised her. "Where are we going?"

"Since I don't know any San Jose restaurants," he chuckled, taking her arm, "I thought we'd go into the city . . ."

"Up to San Francisco?"

"Okay with you? I know a little place near the wharf..."

"Everyone knows a little place near the wharf!" She laughed delightedly. "I warn you, I'm going to order lobster."

"You're just getting even for that chateaubriand," he accused, unlocking the door of the Lotus.

But the mood of the evening had been set and later, overlooking San Francisco bay, Talia ordered her lobster with gusto, throwing in an expensive Napa Valley Chardonnay for good measure.

"Well, you shouldn't have asked my preference," she

said easily as Kane gave the order to the wine steward while shooting her a severe glance.

"I'll remember that next time. Now, about Justin Westbrook," he began.

"Yes." She smiled in anticipation, leaning forward. "Tell me about Justin Westbrook. And then we really have to talk about what we're going to do next. I've had some serious second thoughts about tracking him down, Kane. I don't think I want to lead Pomeroy to him . . ." She broke off with a hint of a frown.

"On the other hand," Kane said quietly, as if he'd been doing some thinking along those lines himself, "perhaps Westbrook should be warned . . ."

That shook her. "About Pomeroy?"

"If he's not who he says he is . . ."

Whatever Kane was going to say next was cut off as a blazingly attractive creature in red swept up to the table, greeting Talia with an exclamation of delight.

"Talia! What luck! You'll never guess what Ralph and I are doing tonight!" The laughing, dark-haired woman turned to the man following close behind and pulled him forward. "Ralph, darling, this is Talia Haywood, my instructor from Advanced Management Designs, remember?"

"How do you do, Talia," a smiling Ralph said warmly, holding out a polite hand. "Gwen's told me a great deal about you."

"Because I owe her so much, of course," Gwen Patton reminded her husband with a chuckle. "I was going to call you in the morning, Talia, and let you know the good news! You'll never believe it, but—"

"You got that promotion, right?" Talia said with a congratulatory smile.

"It was announced today. I've been walking around on air all day and tonight Ralph and I are celebrating. I'm so glad we ran into you. You can join us in a drink." She smiled cheerfully up at Kane, who had risen politely and silently to his feet.

Talia made some quick introductions. "Perhaps you and Ralph could sit down for a minute and have a glass of wine with us?"

"Great." With her usual decisiveness, Gwen was already helping herself to an extra chair and Ralph, with a tiny, slightly apologetic smile, did the same.

"Just think, Talia, I'm finally on my way, thanks to you." Gwen's animated enthusiasm made Talia smile.

"You know full well the sole person responsible for your own success is yourself!" she told her former student firmly.

"That's not true!" Gwen turned to Kane as if seeking to explain something Talia refused to understand. "She's a fantastic instructor, isn't she? I mean, she really knows how to help you get yourself together, channel your energies, get *organized*!"

"Oh, I'm learning a great deal from her," Kane assured the woman with such finesse that Talia barely felt the edge of the knife. She blinked and then glared at him, but he was already deftly leading Gwen Patton through a glowing discussion of Talia's abilities.

"When I started those management training seminars with Talia I had the most incredibly chauvinistic boss, didn't I, Ralph? Poor Ralph, I used to waste hours complaining to him about that man! I was certain I was never going to get anywhere as long as he was in charge. Then Talia showed me how to dissect a situation such as the one I was in—analyze it for the power dynamics involved. The

119

thing to remember is that everyone who holds power is vulnerable. You have to make certain that whoever is in charge understands or senses that the working relationship functions in two directions. He must know that he's ultimately dependent on you and you've got to make that dependency clear in subtle ways."

"Fascinating." Kane threw a loaded glance at Talia, who lowered her eyes quickly to her wineglass. Embarrassment at Gwen's unstinting praise raised bright flags in her cheeks.

"Well, after a couple of weeks under Talia's guidance, I really began getting control of my work environment and the power plays going on in it. Honestly, you should have seen me diagramming out all my working relationships and using all those charts and graphs Talia gives her students." Gwen laughed, shaking her head. "But it works! It really works. A sense of control and the ability to understand and wield power in an effective, honest manner are the two things needed to get to the top. Before I started taking Talia's seminar I wouldn't have dreamed such things could be taught."

"She's got me thinking of signing up for some of A.M.D.'s classes," Ralph confessed. "I had gotten to the point where I was advising her to look for another position, but in a few weeks she completely changed the nature of the one she was in. And here we sit tonight, celebrating a fantastic promotion!" His dark eyes glowed with pride for his wife.

Talia felt compelled to put a brake on all the outpouring of enthusiasm for her classes. She knew the truth, even if no one else had figured it out.

"It wouldn't have mattered how many seminars you attended, Gwen. Nothing would have changed if you

120

hadn't had the basic, underlying strength of will and talent to change it. You're a born manager."

"But what good would talent have done me if I hadn't learned the tricks for controlling it?" Gwen protested with a dismissing wave.

"You'd have picked up what you needed on your own eventually," Talia inserted firmly.

"She's much too modest, isn't she, Mr. Sebastian?" Gwen turned to Kane again for agreement and to Talia's rueful disgust, got it.

"I've never met a woman who could manage quite like Talia," he said cheerfully.

The congratulations and toasts to success went on until Gwen and Ralph finished their glasses of wine and reluctantly rose to move off to their own table. As much as she liked Gwen and wished her well, Talia watched her disappear with a sense of relief.

She accepted with gratitude the small silence that descended over the table, studying the contents of her nearly empty wineglass with great care.

"That woman," Kane finally observed very thoughtfully, "seems to think she owes you all the credit for setting her on the path to success in the business world."

Talia shrugged, not meeting his eyes. "She's got what it takes. She would have made it with or without my classes."

"What, exactly, does she have, Talia?"

The quietly asked question brought her head up and the amber eyes were abruptly snagged in green bonds.

"She's strong, she's intelligent, and she's got guts. She has the strength of will to take hold of a situation and maintain control. If she'd been the one who set out to blackmail you, Kane, you wouldn't have been able to call

121

her bluff. Whether or not she would have gone through with the threats wouldn't have mattered. You'd have *believed* her capable of doing it if she sat in your office and told you that's what she was going to do. You wouldn't have been able to disarm her by seducing her!"

"You're telling me she has something you don't have and that you wish you did?" he murmured.

"If I'd had it, I wouldn't have allowed myself to be crushed by that mess in Sacramento three years ago at Darius & Darnell!"

"Does it occur to you," he went on meditatively, ignoring the barely concealed bitterness in her words, "that you might have another kind of ability? One that's just as valuable? It isn't everyone who could have given that woman the skills she needed to take hold of her career and put it on the right track . . ."

"Kane, I'd rather not discuss this any further," Talia told him repressively. "I'm teaching management instead of practicing it because I don't have the toughness and the sheer guts to make it work in real life. You of all people should know that. When I tried using a power play on you, it was a total disaster—a joke, from your point of view. Now let's forget it, shall we? I want to know about Justin Westbrook."

He hesitated and Talia had the impression he was deliberating whether or not to let her terminate the discussion, which only went to prove her own words, she thought unhappily. She didn't even have the ability to force him off a simple topic of conversation! When it came to wielding power, she seriously doubted that Kane Sebastian had ever needed lessons.

Then he appeared to relent. "All right," he said with a small smile that told her he hadn't forgotten the other

122

subject, merely agreed to shelve it. "I haven't got much, but it's a possibility. I was telling you the truth when I said there was an old contact left down in that town in South America. My firm closed its office there not long after Westbrook, er, left our employ. But the old man we had managing it elected to stay on and retire. I sent the cable to him and I got the answer back this morning. He said he had the impression Westbrook, too, had been planning retirement."

"Retirement!"

"It could be that a man in his unusual occupation has to plan such an event more carefully than other folks," Kane suggested mildly.

Talia couldn't help smiling in response. "Yes, I can see where that might be the case. Coming in from the cold or something like that, hmm?"

"You've definitely read too many espionage thrillers," he sighed. "But, then, I must have too, or I wouldn't be planning to go along with this! At any rate, it seems Westbrook and my ex-manager in South America became friends while they worked together. Perhaps because they were both making plans for the future. The cable I got suggests the possibility of a little town up near the Oregon border . . ." He named a tiny place Talia had never heard of. "George says Westbrook mentioned it a couple of times over tequila. Talked about having a charter fishing boat some day and living the easy life."

Talia grew thoughtful as she considered the information. "It's a possibility all right. A definite possibility. I've checked out far more uncertain leads. Oh, Kane! After all these years! To be so close . . ."

He waited, a strange smile shaping his mouth.

"But what about Pomeroy?" Talia looked at him worriedly.

"It seems likely to me," he said softly, "that your friend Pomeroy might be keeping an eye on your apartment these days. He's probably not too worried about us tonight because we obviously left without any luggage, clearly headed for an evening on the town. He has no reason to think we're going to do anything else except return home afterward. If he does get anxious sometime toward morning, he might bestir himself to check out my motel . . . ."

"But by then we will be long gone?" Talia concluded breathlessly, eyes alight with the taste of adventure as she caught his meaning.

"It's just a suggestion, of course," he demurred modestly. "But there's no reason we couldn't simply continue on up the coast from San Francisco tonight."

Tonight. Talia turned that over in her head. It would mean spending the night with Kane somewhere en route. She would have to be very firm about that particular situation!

But the temptation of solving the riddle of Justin Westbrook was too great to resist.

"Yes," she said softly. "Yes, let's head north tonight."

"I thought the notion might appeal to you," he drawled as the lobster arrived.

There was such satisfaction in his voice that Talia was left with the uncomfortable impression she'd just been neatly maneuvered—again.

But she couldn't bring herself to believe Kane was lying to her. She trusted her instincts far enough to judge that he was telling her the truth about Westbrook's possible location.

So why the sense of unease?

But that really wasn't so hard to answer. People like Kane Sebastian never did anything unless it led to something they wanted. And he wanted her. Did he think that he could have her in exchange for helping her solve her puzzle?

CHAPTER SEVEN

"I don't have anything with me. I'm going to look a little strange wearing this outfit into a small fishing town tomorrow afternoon!" Talia glanced ruefully down at the black and gold dress as she slid into the Lotus after dinner.

"Want to risk going back to get your things?" Kane asked as he got in beside her and started the eager engine.

"Not with that Pomeroy person watching my apartment!" She shivered beneath the gold silk shawl. "Who do you suppose he is, Kane?"

"I have no idea. Like you, I've got some serious doubts about his being with the FBI." He slanted her a faintly amused glance. "Perhaps your friend Westbrook will know."

"Oh, Kane, I hope we're doing the right thing!"

"I don't see that we have much alternative under the circumstances. If we've found Westbrook, it probably won't be long before others do too. If I were him, I'd want to know the trail was getting warm. Ignorance is probably not bliss in his business."

The red Lotus raced easily through the night, across the Golden Gate Bridge and on into Marin County, following Highway 101 north.

For a time silence reigned in the intimate leather cockpit. Talia found herself feeling strangely content with Kane beside her in spite of all she knew about him and about his world. She was deeply attracted to the man regardless of her wariness and in the warm cocoon of the car's interior her feelings were too ambivalent to allow for an organized defense. It was easier to relax and accept the moment.

"What are you thinking about, sitting over there curled up like a cat in the moonlight?" he broke the silence to ask very softly.

"Do you always get fanciful around midnight?"

"Always."

"I was thinking about you," she confessed. "If you'd conceived this brilliant plan a little earlier today, I could have smuggled along a change of clothes!" She grinned pertly, not wanting to admit how intimate her thoughts had become.

"Sorry. It didn't occur to me until dinner. I'm not a fully trained secret agent, remember, able to plot every move in the great chess game well in advance! Complaining already?"

"Not me." She chuckled. "This has to rank as one of the great adventures of my life!"

"I could easily become jealous of Justin Gage West-brook," Kane muttered.

Talia was instantly contrite. "I appreciate what you're doing, Kane. I can't thank you enough—" She broke off

127

as he swung his gaze momentarily from the road to give her a very level glance.

"You know damn well how you can thank me."

Talia's sense of contentment began to vanish. She stared at his profile as he turned his eyes back to the road. Every hard line of his face appeared to be etched in granite.

"You're not being very subtle about it, are you?" she whispered.

"You know the price I'm asking for my services," he stated quietly.

"I haven't said I'll pay it, Kane. We haven't made a . . . a bargain," she reminded him fiercely.

"But you knew what I wanted in exchange for my help," he replied calmly.

"You said today that the information is mine regardless . . ." Damn it! Her voice had an edge to it, an edge that clearly reflected her rasped nerves.

"It is," he agreed. "I'm taking a risk."

"The risk that I'll feel somehow obligated to . . . to pay for your help? Forget it, Kane. I've told you I don't do business that way!" In the faint light of the dash, Talia's chin lifted proudly.

"We'll see," he returned equably, dismissing the subject with a casualness that infuriated her. "Tell me, is there anyone who's going to miss you for the next day or so while you run off looking for adventure?"

"Is that a way of asking if there's any other man in my life?" she retorted, annoyed.

"As you said, I'm not always very subtle."

"Believe it or not, I do lead a relatively normal social life," she bit out caustically.

"I never doubted it for a moment. That's what's worry-

128

ing me," he told her dryly. "Anyone in particular I should know about?"

"I don't intend to discuss you with my other dates, so there's no reason I should discuss them with you."

"Talia!"

Her head came sharply around at the warning note in his voice. "Yes, Kane?"

"Just tell me the truth, okay?" he growled in resignation.

"What do I get in exchange?" she shot back with mocking interest. "A rundown on your girl friends?"

"If that's what you want."

"No, thanks!" A businessman! Always willing to bargain!

She could almost feel him drawing the rein on his patience. When he spoke again, his voice was astonishingly cool with a deep certainty buried in it.

"You know what I think? I think there isn't anyone else. No one serious, that is. Why don't you admit it, honey? You couldn't have given yourself to me so completely the way you did that night if there was another man in your life. You're not the type."

"You think I'm too weak to juggle a couple of men in my life at the same time? You don't think I have enough of the female buccaneer in me to take my pleasures where and when I wish?" she demanded.

"I think," he retorted, "that you're too gentle, too honest, and too vulnerable to take those kinds of emotional risks."

"In other words, I don't have the guts to take what I want from life!"

"You'll get what you want from life," he murmured, "but you won't use the same tactics harder people use."

"What about you?" she shot back flippantly, anxious to change the focus of what was becoming a most uncomfortable conversation. "Anyone I should be jealous of?"

"If I thought it would encourage you, I'd invent a dozen beauties to tease you about! The truth is, I haven't thought of anyone else since the day you walked into my office. Maybe even before that. There was something in those letters of yours that intrigued me. Why do you think I bothered to let you make an appointment in the first place?"

"I had to force myself on your secretary!"

He shook his head, grinning. "I'm the one who told her to go ahead and set up the appointment. But I instructed her to make things a little difficult. I wanted you a bit anxious, I suppose—"

"So you'd have a psychological advantage? I should have known. Talk about power dynamics! Kane, I want to get something very clear between us. Our . . . agreement to give this relationship another chance doesn't mean we're going to pick up where we left off that night in your home! I want to make sure you understand that," she announced gravely.

"Better start looking for a motel, sweetheart," he said gently, ignoring her warning. "It's getting late and we've already put plenty of miles behind us."

She knew he didn't intend to respond to her attempt at creating a firm understanding between them. As the initial excitement of the adventure began to wear off, it occurred to Talia that she might find her hands full trying to manage Kane. Her track record to date was rather poor.

In the end, it was Kane who made the motel selection. He decided on a pleasant, modern place beside the highway, which was still flashing a VACANCY sign.

"They've even got a machine that dispenses tooth-brushes," he grinned, coming back to the car after registering. "Tomorrow morning we can get you some jeans and sandals in town."

Talia climbed out of the Lotus, stifling a yawn. "If you'll give me my key, I'll be on my way. I'm exhausted."

"This way."

He started off in the direction of a second-floor room overlooking the silent swimming pool. Ushering her inside, he turned and closed the door behind them with a finality that told her everything she needed to know.

"Don't scream," he begged wryly. "I didn't have any choice."

"You're going to tell me there was only one room?" she inquired acidly.

Kane yanked wearily at his tie, stalking toward the second of two double beds and sinking down onto it. "At least I managed two beds. Don't I get any credit for that?"

"Kane!"

"Talia, listen to me," he sighed. "Neither of us really knows what we're doing. We've got to exercise a little caution. What if we didn't succeed in shaking Pomeroy tonight? Hell, I'm not an expert at ditching tails. I'm no James Bond! The only safe thing to do until we find Westbrook is stick together. Pomeroy might do something drastic if he realizes what we're up to at the moment."

Talia stood glaring fiercely at him while she considered that, knowing she was beaten before she began. Kane had made up his mind. Short of walking out of the room . . .

"Forget it," he advised smoothly, watching the play of emotions racing across her face. "This really was the last room they had!"

The worst part about the whole thing was that she believed him! And he might have a point about Pomeroy. Grimly she extended her hand.

He glanced at the outstretched palm questioningly.

"May I please have one of those toothbrushes you bought?" she asked sweetly.

Without a word he handed one over. "You believe me?" he asked as she started toward the bath.

"I believe that if I go down to the front desk and ask for a second room I'll be told there isn't one available," she replied as she stepped into the tiled bathroom and started to close the door. "You're not the sort to leave loose ends." She closed the door a little violently.

When she emerged, Kane was waiting for his turn, stripped to the waist, shoes lying on the carpet beside the bed he'd chosen. The intimate sight of his smoothly muscled chest with its cloud of inviting, curly red hair brought back far too many memories. She knew an impulse to once again entwine her hands through that hair, seek out the flat, masculine nipples . . . She turned aside as he paced past her.

"A word of advice," she thought to say just before he closed the bathroom door. He paused politely. "Don't drink out of either one of those glasses of water on the sink. I've got my contacts soaking in them."

"What happens," he asked wickedly, "if I reverse the glasses?"

"Don't you dare!" she yelped, thinking of the uncomfortableness which would ensue if she inserted the left lens into the right eye the next morning. Things would have been much simpler if she'd had some warning about this little escapade.

She scrambled into bed, removing the black dress under

132

the covers and feeling like an idiot. She left on only the lacy bra and panties. Then she turned out the light.

Kane emerged into a discreetly darkened room and she curled on her side, facing the wall as he groped his way toward his bed.

"Damn!"

The muffled, forceful exclamation preceded by a dull thud brought Talia's head around.

"What in the world!"

He was bending over, massaging one foot. In the moonlight she could see he was wearing only a pair of briefs. The dark chestnut head lifted, and even in the shadows Talia caught the glitter of the green eyes.

"Are you all right?" Talia asked anxiously.

"No! But I don't suppose it matters to you if I never walk again!"

"Lucky you have a nice car for transportation, huh?" she murmured innocently, amused even though she was sorry about his injured toe.

"You're a cruel woman," he complained, limping his way to the bed and crawling under the covers.

"I'm practicing to become tough like you and Gwen Patton."

"You wouldn't, by any chance, care to view a few slides before going to sleep, would you?" he drawled invitingly.

"No, thanks, I learned my lesson. Never accept a man's invitation to look at dirty pictures!"

"Dirty pictures! I resent that! A few may have been a bit smudged, but . . . Hey!"

"What now?"

The sudden rustling of bedclothing made Talia glance once more over her shoulder. "Kane? Where are you going?"

She stared in amazement as he pulled on his slacks and reached for the keys to the Lotus.

"Pictures! I knew I'd seen your friend Pomeroy somewhere!"

Before she could question him further, he was gone, slipping out the motel door and closing it after him. Talia sat tensely, sheet clutched to her breast, waiting for him to return.

When he did, he was triumphantly waving a small packet. "Look at these." He switched on the lamp beside her bed, sinking down on the mattress and scattering the photos in the small envelope.

Talia glanced down at the pictures strewn across the blanket, terribly aware of Kane's proximity. There she was in scene after scene. Some of the shots were excellent, others made her groan. But in two or three Aaron Pomeroy could be detected in the background.

"That bastard followed us all over town," Kane muttered softly.

"Well, if we do find Justin tomorrow, we'll have these to show him. Maybe he'll recognize Pomeroy."

Kane nodded, slowly collecting the photos. "Not bad, hmm?" he demanded, pausing over the one of her petting the bored horse.

"Who? Me or the horse?"

"The whole thing! The composition, the lighting, the artful pose . . . Talia, I've got to at least kiss you good night. I'm going to go out of my mind as it is, having you so near and not being able to hold you!"

He was too close. By the time the sudden, dangerous timber of his voice had registered, the situation was too far along to control. Before she could do more than say his name defensively, he was gathering her into his arms, crushing her back against the pillows.

Her protest was a muffled thing, swallowed up in his throat as he covered her mouth with his own. He used his weight without any compunction to trap her there amid the sheets, his thigh thrown across her legs, pinning them.

"Talia, Talia . . ."

Although he held her so completely, his mouth moved on hers with the seductive, half-demanding, half-pleading urgency she remembered so well. It was a caress that called to every nerve and fiber of her being, reminding her of all she had tried to forget.

Using his thumb, Kane probed at the corner of her mouth, urging apart her lips and plunging into the honeyed interior when she surrendered that first, small step.

In spite of all her determination to stay in control of herself and of him, Talia felt the passion flare to life with the heat and energy of a raging fire. It surged through her body, setting alight every particle of her being.

Kane's hands snagged in her loosened hair, anchoring her twisting head as he sought to master her mouth completely. Only when she moaned softly and the fingers digging into the muscles of his shoulders began moving in deep, circular motions did he free her head to find the edge of the sheet that separated them. He moved his lips to lick the curve of her neck.

"No, Kane! I swore I wouldn't let you do this to me again . . ."

"I'm not doing anything to you! You're doing it to me! Don't you realize that, yet, little one? Do you think I wanted it to be this way? Do you think I planned to wind up chasing after you, offering you the only lure I had at my command in an effort to tempt you back into my arms?"

Talia's breath hissed between her teeth as he nipped erotically at the skin of her shoulder. The thought of holding any power over him at all was utterly intoxicating, she discovered. Had it really happened the way he implied? Had he been forced against his will to pursue her because of what he'd found in her arms the night he'd attempted to teach her a lesson?

"Let me make love to you, Talia," he commanded hoarsely, pulling down the sheet in small increments. "Let me love you the way you did that night. The memory of the way you gave yourself to me has kept me awake nights since then!"

Hot sensuous kisses followed the retreating edge of the sheet, each one leaving the fire blazing higher and higher. Talia twisted beneath him, her body seeking his, and she found the curling hair at the back of his neck.

She couldn't answer. The memory had haunted her too, because it had seemed to her at the time that the giving had been mutual that night. It was only afterward that she had been shown the truth and made to feel a fool. Now here he was, begging for the warmth and tenderness she'd given him once before.

Begging or demanding? With Kane it was hard to tell!

"Don't fight me, Talia. I'll take care of you. You won't regret it." Her bra seemed to float free of her body at his touch.

"You said that once before," she managed huskily as he lowered the sheet to her waist and let the curling roughness of his chest hair rasp her nipples into taut peaks. He knew so much about making her body respond, she thought dizzily. Had he learned her so well that first night?

"Talia!" he groaned, circling one sensitive nipple with his finger in a random little pattern that made her shiver. He bent to kiss the evidence of her rising passion. "It didn't have to end like that. If you hadn't run off . . ."

"I could have stuck around and listened to your egotistical lectures?" she finished for him, torn with a fierce yearning to either surrender or hurt him. Perhaps both. And she had so little power.

"I'm here," he soothed. "I came after you, didn't I? I brought you what you wanted . . ."

"And you expect me to sleep with you in exchange for it!" she hissed, her senses whirling as she plunged to the decision.

"No . . ." he began. Then, "Hell, yes! I want you too badly to deny it!"

"It's all right, Kane," she got out throatily, touching her fingers to his mouth as he raised his head. She looked at him through her lashes, knowing she was going to go ahead with what she had decided. "It's all right. I accept the bargain."

Above her silencing finger the green eyes glittered with a startling fire. But it wasn't only passion blazing forth from the jeweled depths. There was a sudden, unexpected anger there too. It stormed over her as she lay in his arms, unresisting.

"Why are you looking at me like that?" she whispered, feeling trapped beneath the tension-filled strength in him. "It's what you wanted. I'm agreeing to what you wanted!"

"No," he grated tightly, his hand splaying possessively across the smooth skin of her stomach. "No, you're not,

137

you little witch. But I'll take it. I'll take whatever I can get!"

With a small, unintelligible cry he lifted himself away from her long enough to uncover her body completely. And then he fumbled impatiently with the buckle of his belt. The slacks wound up in a careless heap on the carpet beside the bed, followed quickly by the single garment Talia had left.

Then he rolled onto his back, pulling her in a sprawl across his chest.

"If it's a *bargain* we have," he growled, his hands tightly gripping her waist, "then we must both be certain we get full value! Make love to me, Talia Haywood. Make love to me as if you meant it!"

Confused, her mind in chaos over Kane's unexpected anger, Talia reacted almost instinctively. Gently, a little hesitantly at first and then with growing sureness, she did as he ordered, seeking to pacify him and turn him back into the man who only moments before had been pleading for her love.

She let the warmth in her pour over him. She loved him. She knew it in the very core of her and it frightened her a little to think ahead to the day when he realized the full extent of his power over her. Better by far that he think she was merely agreeing to her side of the "bargain."

And so, because she could not tell him of her love, she gave it to him in the only way left open. With touch and heat and movement she sought to trigger the desire in him, to douse the devil of anger that had appeared in those gleaming green eyes and replace it with need and want.

Her tawny hair brushed across his hard chest and taut stomach as she rained kisses along his hair-rough skin.

Every groan, every tightening of his hands in her hair or on her shoulders was another small accomplishment, a little victory to be treasured.

She gently raked the inside of his leg with the tips of her nails, delighting in the sudden surge of response in him. Her lips feathered the whole waiting length of him from throat to ankle and then returned to explore the sensitive pit of his stomach.

"Talia! My God, Talia! You have me half out of my mind!"

She caught the hardness of his manhood in a soft, loving embrace and heard him cry out with the desire she had wanted so badly to elicit.

Then, as if she had pushed him beyond some vital limit, he seized her hips with rough tenderness and pushed her onto her back. Broad shoulders lifted beside her as Kane paused and fumbled briefly in the darkness. She knew what he was doing and it touched her that he took the responsibility without question. He was a man who could be trusted, she thought dazedly, in more ways than one.

When he came to her, moving with silent urgency, she opened her arms as she had that first night. There were no reservations, no holding back. She wanted him and he wanted her. On that level, at least, the bargain was an equal one.

She cried out softly as he drew a hand slowly down the whole of her body, her breath catching in her throat. Gently he stroked her until she writhed and twisted beneath him.

"Please, Kane, please . . ."

"Do you want me now, little witch?" he demanded deeply against the skin of her breast.

"Yes, please. Oh, Kane, I . . . I want you so much." He didn't seem to notice the hesitancy in her voice as she stumbled to change the word *love* to *want*.

"Are you content with your bargain?" he prodded, using his knee to separate her legs. Slowly he lowered himself to her body as if he were sampling a priceless wine.

She didn't understand the question. It was as if he wanted her to answer in the negative! But there was no time to question, no time to analyze. The passion raged between them too fiercely, demanding satisfaction.

"I accept what you're offering," she whispered shakily, looking up at him with heavy-lidded eyes as she circled his neck with her arms.

"And I shall have to be content with what I can get in return, is that it?"

She stared up at him, not understanding his tension as he held himself poised above her.

"It's what you wanted," she reminded him softly. "It's all you wanted."

"No, it's not. But I'll take it. I'll take it."

And then he was completing the passionate union, merging totally with her in a way that made her body sing. Her fingertips dug ecstatically into his back. Her whole being flamed with the excitement and wonder of the embrace.

"Talia!"

She clung to him, her fingers seeking a new and tighter purchase. He slid his hands under her hips, lifting her to him as he called out her name.

Together they spiraled through the rarified atmosphere of the physical bonding that had begun that first night. The electricity of it sparked around them, in them. It charged and recharged them both, whipping them toward the ultimate explosion.

When it came, Talia gave herself up to it freely, knowing that in doing so she was, in reality, giving herself freely into Kane's keeping for as long as he wanted her.

CHAPTER EIGHT

The paper bag containing the new jeans and a brushed cotton plaid shirt came sailing toward the partially opened bathroom door. Talia barely managed to catch it, struggling as she was to hold a large white towel around her shower-damp body at the same time.

"Are you always this grouchy in the mornings?" She frowned across the room. The night had been a time of enchantment. The morning after had been filled with a brooding tension that made Talia feel as if she were walking on eggs. Her nerves were already on edge and it was still early. What had gone wrong? She'd been asking herself that for an hour.

"You'll be finding out all about my morning habits, won't you?"

Kane didn't look at her as he investigated the contents of another sack he'd brought back with him from his trip to the nearby town. He was dressed in jeans, Western-cut shirt, this one in yellow, and a pair of boots, all of which he had luckily left in the car when he'd checked into the motel in San Jose.

"I'm not sure I want to find out," Talia told him crisply, rapidly becoming annoyed. Her brows drew together into a line of disapproval that she hoped masked her inner state of nerves. What was wrong with him this morning? What had she done? Was he regretting his bargain already? "You've been snapping at me since you woke up! As the female in this little duo, I'd like to remind you that I'm the one who's supposed to be having regrets about a one-night-stand!"

He reacted as if she'd just thrown down a gauntlet. Pausing abruptly in the act of snapping off the lid of a plastic coffee cup, Kane lifted glittering green eyes to meet hers. The tension that had been circulating in the room for the past hour coalesced into something much more menacing. Talia's hand tightened on the edge of the door.

"I knew it!" he gritted out, gliding toward her with the coffee cup still in one hand. "I knew that's what you were thinking! But it's too late, Talia. Our bargain was for a second chance, not just one night in bed. You made the deal of your own free will. Don't think you can start amending it. You gave yourself to me last night and I'm retaining possession. This afternoon I make the first and only required payment!"

"*If* we find Westbrook!" Talia tossed back bravely, a little frightened of the cold intent she read in him. What was wrong with him? Didn't he understand the binding nature of the bond he had forged last night? Whatever his uncertainties about her sticking around until he'd received satisfaction in their "bargain," he had no right to intimidate her like this.

"There are no *ifs* about it," he told her with silky men-

143

ace as he reached the bathroom door and pushed it open. "My sole obligation is to take you to Westbrook's last known address. Whether or not we find him doesn't change your side of the deal!"

Talia backed up, amber eyes wary. She felt as if she were sharing the small space with a green-eyed panther. Last night he had been alternately tender, masterful, exciting, teasing, fiercely passionate. He had brought her again and again to a shivering completion in his arms and he knew it. She had thought him equally satisfied. What was wrong?

"Okay, Kane, I give up," she tried to say pertly as she came up against the white tile wall. "Why are you trying to intimidate me? Why the heavy-handed, aggressive male act this morning?"

"Stop labeling my actions as if they fit into your lecture number three-fifteen on chauvinistic bosses!" he exploded. "It's not an act, damn it. I *am* feeling aggressive. And territorial. And all the other things a man feels at a time like this. It's got nothing to do with corporate politics or power dynamics in the boardroom! It's a whole hell of a lot more primitive and you, by God, are supposed to become meek and submissive in response!"

Talia blinked at the sheer masculine frustration washing over her and wanted to laugh but didn't quite dare. As if he sensed her wish, Kane lifted his hands to the sides of her throat. They curled gently but firmly around her skin.

"This is my meek and submissive smile, see?" she said with a shaky attempt at humor. "Now you're supposed to calm down and cease the veiled threats. Haven't you studied dominant-submissive behavior among the apes?"

"And if I don't cease my apelike behavior?" he inquired

144

very politely, green eyes responding reluctantly to the amusement in her.

"Then I will have no recourse but to dump this glass of cold water over your head." She lifted one of the glasses that had held her contact lenses overnight. The lens had already been safely removed and inserted into her eye. "It would be a shame to get that nice pearl-buttoned shirt all wet. Very uncomfortable for driving, I should imagine."

"Talk about threats and intimidation!"

"I'm learning."

"Talia," he groaned, his hands on the nape of her neck pressing her against the front of his shirt with abrupt urgency. "I have to know what you think you're going to do after I've paid off my half of the deal! Are you going to run again?"

She inhaled his pleasant morning scent, finding it enticing. It was compounded of the soap from the small shaving kit he'd purchased in the lobby, the freshness of his shower, and the indefinable tang that was *him*.

"Is that what this is really all about?" she whispered in a muffled voice against the yellow shirt. "You're afraid I won't stick around to pay my half?"

"It occurred to me sometime during the small hours of the morning," he began dryly, "that it wasn't going to take your analytical brain long to realize that after I deliver you to Westbrook's location, I no longer have a hold on you."

Didn't have a hold on her! It was difficult to credit Kane Sebastian with such a lack of perception! Still, this uncertainty in him was her only defense against the power in him. She would be a fool to surrender that defense completely. Kane would have no compunction about taking everything she had to give. If she offered her love, he would grab it, seeing it as a far more tangible chain than

145

the one he held through having found Westbrook's possible whereabouts.

"You'll just have to have a little faith in my business integrity, won't you?" she quipped.

"Talia!"

His growl reminded her once more of a panther. She relented slightly, pulling back to meet his eyes.

"Kane, I understand the bargain. I understood it when I made it last night. I'm . . . I'm willing to give us a second chance."

He stared down at her, eyes hooded and brooding. The fingers at the nape of her neck kneaded restlessly. "I'm going to have to be satisfied with that?" Kane asked.

"It's what you asked for," she reminded him evenly.

His face hardened. "You'd better believe I'm going to make damn sure you deliver full value. If you've got any notion at all of skipping out on me after today—"

"You're going to threaten to come after me again with more photographs with which to seduce me?" Talia demanded.

"You're not going to be serious about this, are you?" Kane retorted.

Talia shrugged, clinging to her flippant attitude because she knew it was all she had left. "I realize those of you in the real business world can't afford a sense of humor, but those of us on the sidelines find it very useful occasionally. It's getting late, Kane."

Instead of answering, he swooped to take her lips in a rough, claim-staking kiss that left her limp and breathless. When he felt her body relax placatingly against his and was convinced of the submission in her response, he released her and stalked out of the bathroom.

* * *

146

Tense watchfulness filled the Lotus for the rest of the trip. Talia had the impression Kane was expecting her to jump out of the car and run off into the distance. She couldn't understand his wariness, but she deliberately did nothing to dull it. A woman in her position, she continually reminded herself, needed whatever psychological assistance she could get. Once Kane fully realized the extent of his power over her she would be lost.

Such thoughts did not go far toward alleviating her own growing unease. The closer they got to the small town on the northern California coast the more nervous she became.

"You haven't said a word for over an hour," Kane observed finally, not lifting his eyes from the now winding coastal highway. On their left the Pacific crashed and roared on the cliffs below.

"You haven't been overly chatty either," she reminded him tartly.

"Worried about not finding Westbrook?" he hazarded to say, his voice gentling a bit.

"Oh, Kane. It's so hard to believe we might be getting close. After all these years! I'm more afraid of finding him than of not finding him, to tell you the truth!"

He hesitated. "Want to change your mind? It's not too late—"

"No! I can't bring myself to quit at this point!"

"Then stop working yourself up into a nervous wreck!"

"Don't snap at me. It only makes me more nervous!"

He grinned wryly, slanting her a quick glance. "I'm probably snapping at you because I'm also nervous!"

His admission released some of the heightening tension and Talia gave him a tremulous little smile. "Worried

147

Westbrook might sue your company for not protecting his privacy?" Talia asked.

"I've got other concerns at the moment." He hesitated and then said very slowly, "Will you be terribly disappointed if we don't find any trace of him, Talia?"

"It will be amazing if we do find him, won't it? I mean, a man like Justin Westbrook has had a lot of experience keeping a low profile."

"Exactly."

"What are you trying to do? Prepare me for the worst?" she demanded lightly.

"This town is the only lead I've got for you. If it doesn't pan out . . ."

She swung around in the seat to look at him with sudden suspicion. "You don't expect it to pan out, do you?"

"Not really." He sighed ruefully. "It's a very thin lead, Talia. But . . ."

"But you did your best to encourage me to follow it because it was all you had to bargain with, right?"

He shrugged under her accusing glare. "As you said, it was all I had."

"Kane, are you telling me you didn't bargain with me in good faith?"

"The lead is valid as far as it goes," he muttered stonily, his eyes firmly on the road.

Talia sat back in the seat, knowing she wasn't going to get anything more out of him. And her case of nerves grew along with the suspense.

The town was a small, sleepy place set on the cliffs and tumbling down to the harbor. Weather-beaten buildings and houses clung determinedly to the areas nearest the water and more architecturally interesting Victorian

148

homes rose above them, seeking a view instead of direct confrontation with the sea.

Talia studied everything with ravening interest. "What shall we do, Kane? Go through the phone book?"

"Forget it," he advised. "I already tried that."

She glanced at him in surprise. "No Westbrooks listed in Directory Assistance?"

"Did you think there would be?" He smiled quirkingly. "He wanted privacy, remember?"

"I guess we could try asking people about a man who might have moved to town within the past couple of years . . ." she suggested slowly. It was beginning to dawn on her that Kane had rushed her off so quickly last night there had been very little chance to organize a realistic search strategy. How did one go about finding a man when one no longer even had much of a description to go on?

"The first thing we're going to do is find a place to stay. It won't be long before sundown, and motels in a place like this are probably a bit scarce."

Impatient as she was to get started on the search, Talia couldn't deny the truth of his statement. The thought of checking into another motel with Kane Sebastian, however, was as unnerving as the thought of possibly being in the same town as Justin Westbrook.

But it wasn't a motel the gas station attendant kindly pointed out—it was a charming old Victorian inn. A former mansion constructed by a ship's captain, it had been turned into a picturesque hotel and was run by a middle-aged couple whose curiosity was friendly and overt.

The cheerful, gray-haired woman behind the front desk took one look at Talia's ringless finger and smiled challengingly up at Kane.

"You'll be wanting two rooms, I take it?"

"My wife and I," he retorted very smoothly, "will only require one room."

Talia winced, turning away as if to study the old Victorian mantel above the fireplace. Behind her she could sense the small battle of wills being conducted over the inn's register. She wasn't surprised when it turned out to be the proprietress who backed down.

"Very well," she declared in defeat, "I have a lovely room on the second floor overlooking the harbor."

"That will be fine."

Twenty minutes later, when Kane carried the one small suitcase he'd happened to have in the car upstairs to the corner room, Talia followed in icy silence.

"Now what's wrong?" he demanded, setting the overnight bag down on the polished hardwood floor and turning to confront her.

But Talia was staring at the huge four-poster bed that occupied most of the room. An old handmade comforter served as blanket and bedspread. In the corner of the room a rock fireplace waited for the match that would ignite the already laid fire. A huge wardrobe, obviously designed by the same craftsman who had constructed the bed, stood against the opposite wall and a charming fainting couch took advantage of the harbor view.

"Nothing," she finally retorted with a false brightness, surveying the room and averting her eyes from the dynasty-founding bed.

"Talia Haywood, sometimes you . . ." Kane began threateningly, his hands going to his lean hips in an impatiently aggressive gesture.

"You mean Talia Sebastian, don't you?" she said sweetly.

"So that's it. What was I supposed to do? That bored

150

motel clerk last night couldn't have cared less, but Mrs. Stanton here looked like she was prepared to fill in as your disapproving aunt!"

"I don't want to argue about it," Talia said primly, knowing she had no real right to protest. She had known what it would mean to agree to Kane's terms. "I just do not like being caught up in lies of convenience. Especially someone else's convenience!"

"I seem to remember you were willing enough to use a few social lies yourself in the recent past," he grated. She thought he was going to take hold of her, but at the look of chagrin on her face he nodded instead, clearly changing his mind. Damn the man! He knew he'd won again.

"At least the place has its own bath," he went on conversationally. "Sometimes in these quaint old places you wind up sharing the one down the hall."

Talia stared at his back, not knowing whether to be resentful or grateful for the change of topic. She decided to busy herself with unpacking her black and gold dress, the only change of wardrobe she had with her.

"I've been thinking," she said over her shoulder, eager to show she could get off the subject of fake marriages as quickly as he could, "maybe we should start down at the harbor. Your ex-manager mentioned something about Justin wanting to set up a small charter fishing business, right?"

"Sounds like as good a place to start as any."

When Talia stepped out of the red Lotus some time later it was to the sound of a distant wolf whistle that emanated from one of the many fishing boats bobbing near the docks. She ignored it, but Kane reached out and firmly took her hand in a possessive manner.

"Don't look at him, for God's sake!" he hissed under his breath. "It only encourages them!"

"It's your own fault for buying me such tight jeans," she chuckled, her sense of humor rising to the fore.

"I bought the size you told me to buy! Next time I'll buy a size larger!"

"Kane, I'm really getting nervous."

"Relax. The odds are we're not going to turn up anything anyhow." He soothed her at once.

"I have a feeling about this . . ."

"You're letting your imagination run away with you," he teased.

She knew he was making an effort to reassure her. Suddenly very grateful for the support he was offering, Talia's fingers tightened within his. He squeezed back and his smile was warm and gentle.

"I guess I never got this far in my imagination," she confessed. "I never stopped to think what I would say to him if I actually found him."

They started toward the planked docking, studying the rows of boats, large and small, tied up at the side. The town boasted a sizeable fishing fleet, Talia realized.

"Want to start at the first boat and ask a few questions?" Kane suggested.

"No . . . Let's just walk around for a bit."

"I thought you'd be racing up to the first person we saw demanding that he point out Justin Westbrook's boat. What happened to that dynamic little blackmailer who confronted me?"

"Stop teasing me. I'm anxious enough as it is."

He pulled her close, releasing her hand to cradle an arm around her waist. "Okay, honey. We'll stroll around a bit until you get your nerve up to ask the questions we came here to ask."

Slowly, as if they were idle tourists, Talia and Kane wandered the gently floating docks, nodding politely to the several men working in the area.

"Would you recognize him?" Talia whispered at one point.

"I never met him. I was paid a very formal call by the man he reported to and the situation was explained to me. I was asked if I would agree to have him put on the payroll and I said yes. The beginning and end of my career in the spy business, I'm afraid."

"Oh."

"What about you?"

"It's been so many years and I haven't seen him since I was very small. No. I wouldn't recognize him."

"Well, we'll just keep our eyes open for someone who looks like a retired spy." Kane chuckled.

They were nearly to the end of the fourth dock when Talia, who had been idly reading boat names, suddenly came to a halt, staring.

"What's wrong, honey?"

"Kane," she whispered, more shaken than she would have believed, "the name on that boat . . ."

He followed her gaze. "The *Allison Lee?* Mean anything to you?"

Before she could respond, a man emerged from the main cabin of the large blue and white boat that had obviously been outfitted for sport fishing. A man in his sixties, there was a wiry toughness about the still trim body. Silver hair, which had once been almost black, was nearly hidden under a woven fishing cap. He wore stained faded denims and a flannel shirt and on his left wrist a gold watch glittered in the fading sun, a jarring note of luxury.

He swept the silent couple on the dock beside his boat with a glance that quickly turned polite and mildly hopeful. But not before Talia had seen something else in that steel gaze. Just for an instant there had been a penetrating watchfulness that would have been unnerving in large doses.

"You folks looking to line up a little fishing?" the man inquired cheerfully, standing on his deck with a negligent pose that spelled a deep self-assurance. Talia had seen that kind of assurance in Kane and she knew it stemmed from an uncompromising inner sense of control.

For another instant the three of them faced each other, the fisherman waiting with grave politeness for his visitors to state their request.

Beside her Kane waited silently, his arm gripping her waist so tightly she knew he was aware of what she was going through. Talia studied the roughly hewn, tanned and weathered face of the older man, trying desperately to remember.

"Did you . . . did you love her very much?" she finally whispered. The evening breeze off the ocean whipped the loosened tendrils of tawny brown hair around her tautly drawn features.

As if she had turned a key in a lock, the easygoing politeness faded from the gray eyes as they met hers. There was a long silence.

"Allison Lee?"

"Yes," she murmured, hardly daring to speak.

"She was," he stated in careful, measured tones, "my best friend's wife. I made certain she never knew how I felt. Yes, I loved her." He waited.

"I'm Talia," she said simply. "Allison Lee was my mother." There was nothing else to say.

She saw him stiffen, his eyes almost piercing in their sudden intensity. "Talia? Talia Haywood?"

She nodded, grateful for the support of Kane's arm.

"Cameron's daughter," Justin Westbrook stated unbelievingly. He reached out a hand as if to touch her and Kane released his grip so that Talia could step into the older man's arms.

"I'm Kane Sebastian," Kane murmured, meeting Westbrook's eyes over Talia's head. "A, uh, former employer of yours. And I hate to put a damper on this touching little reunion, but we may have brought some trouble along with us. Ever hear of a man named Aaron Pomeroy?"

CHAPTER NINE

"Pomeroy is a bungler," announced Justin Westbrook a long time later as he sat with Kane and Talia in the cozy dining room of the old inn. "But even bunglers have their uses. He's a low-level double agent I stumbled across a few years ago. He reports to a small but rather aggressive Middle Eastern nation that likes to think it has a line into United States security. It was decided to leave him in place and feed him the sort of information the Department wanted that particular Middle Eastern country to have."

"A double agent!" Talia breathed, entranced.

"Don't mind her," Kane instructed the older man glibly. "She reads a lot of espionage thrillers."

Justin laughed while Talia shot Kane an evil glance over a spoonful of Mrs. Stanton's homemade clam chowder.

"Pomeroy knows I know about him. He thinks I'm the only one who does, so it proved convenient to have him believe me dead. There were a few other folks running around the world at the time who I knew would rest easier if they thought me dead too. So"—he shrugged in the shirt and tie he'd managed to find for dinner—"it seemed the simplest way to retire."

Kane reached out and scooped up the photographs he'd been showing to Justin. "Nobody ever instructed me to destroy the records of your employment," he said musingly. "Perhaps I should have on my own?"

"Absolutely not! My time with your company was supposed to look legitimate and aboveboard," Justin assured him. Then he grinned in sudden reminiscence. "Besides, it was. Didn't I get that valve order for you from that drilling firm?"

"That's right, you did. I'd forgotten about that. I had a good laugh over it when it came through the purchasing department! I don't believe I ever had a chance to thank you."

Justin waved the gratitude aside. "It was the least I could do. You did the Department a favor by agreeing to take me on the payroll. McCary had approached a couple of other firms before he got to yours and no one wanted to take the risks of providing cover for a government agent in South America. Bad for the public image if it ever got out, you know," he added dryly.

"I know," Kane agreed, equally dryly. He lifted a quelling eyebrow at Talia, who ignored him. He'd more than gotten even for her attempt at blackmail. She wasn't about to be made to feel guilty now!

"So you believed the reports of my death to be greatly exaggerated, hmm?" Justin smiled at Talia as he worked on a crab leg. "My respects for your intuition. I can't believe you actually found me. How long did it take you, following all those buried leads?"

"It's been a hobby of mine for years. Ever since Dad was

157

killed, in fact." She hurried on as she saw the momentary cloud in the steel eyes. They'd already been through that painful subject. "I suppose I started looking because there was something about the whole thing that fascinated me."

"You don't have to explain," Justin said quietly. "I understand."

"You do?"

"Sure. There's something about following a trail to the end. It gets in your blood. What did you think when Pomeroy started asking questions yesterday?"

"I didn't know what to think at first. I just knew there was something very wrong about him."

"Good instincts," Justin approved with a quick grin. "It never occurred to you he might be telling the truth? That I might not be one of the good guys in the white hats?"

"Of course not!" Talia was shocked.

"What about you, Kane?" Justin asked interestedly.

Kane looked at him levelly for a moment and then the corners of his mouth quirked upward. "Oh, I figured Pomeroy was probably up to no good as soon as Talia told me about him."

"Because you trust Talia's instincts?"

"I have the greatest respect for Talia's instincts, but . . ." He paused, glancing ruefully at her. "I had a little more to go on than that. You see, when the answer to my cable came back, I started worrying."

"About what would happen if you actually did find me?" Justin smiled understandingly.

"Exactly. So I did a little digging and finally got a call through to McCary, your old boss."

"Ah!"

"Kane! You didn't! Why on earth . . . ?" Talia turned on him, thoroughly annoyed.

158

"Don't get mad, honey. I just wanted to make certain you weren't going to walk into anything you couldn't handle. I really didn't expect to find Justin, but I knew you'd insist on checking out this town. What if he did turn up and what if there were reasons he shouldn't be found?"

"And what did this . . . this McCary person tell you?" she demanded.

"Oh, he maintained Justin was dead, but when I asked him a hypothetical question—"

"What hypothetical question?" She interrupted, irritated at not having been told about Kane's efforts.

"Something along the lines of what would happen if my charming, persistent fiancée managed to turn up a not-quite-dead Justin Westbrook—"

"Fiancée!" Talia's stared at him, her irritation turning into outright anger. *"Fiancée!"* Kane and his social lies!

Kane smiled blandly at her and turned to Justin. "In answer to my hypothetical question, McCary assured me that the United States Government had no objections whatsoever to your running around on the loose. That you had served your country well and certainly deserved a quiet retirement. Unfortunately at the time I didn't know about Pomeroy, so I couldn't inquire about him."

"Justin, what if we've led him to you?" Talia asked, abruptly worried again.

"Relax, Talia. How could you know that one of your many letters of inquiry would wind up on his desk and set him off?" Justin soothed her. "In any event, I think Aaron Pomeroy's usefulness has probably come to an end anyway. I don't think McCary is going to be too upset if it becomes necessary to terminate his employment with the Department."

"Terminate!" Talia stared at him.

"She has got an active imagination, hasn't she?" Justin pointed out to Kane.

"I tried to warn you."

Westbrook turned back to Talia, amusement dancing in the steel-colored eyes. "Don't worry, my dear. Most spies, like most businessmen, die in bed at an advanced age. Blowing Pomeroy's cover would be all that is necessary to neutralize him."

"I see," she said a little weakly, feeling foolish.

"A little matter which I will take care of tomorrow with a phone call to McCary. It won't take long. Pomeroy will soon find it convenient to leave the country. I don't want him hanging around bothering either of us!

"Pretty sharp of you to suspect him from the beginning, though. But, then, I'd expect any kid of Cameron and Allison's to be sharp. What did you say you did for a living?"

"She teaches seminars in management to people like me," Kane explained, digging out a clam from the pile in front of him. "And she's damn good at it. Just ask one of her students."

"You're a student of hers?"

"Kane never needed lessons in that subject," Talia declared firmly. "He's a natural. I wasn't and that's why I teach it. Enough about me. I want to talk about you, Justin. Why did you lose touch with us? Mom and Dad thought you were dead."

The older man met her eyes across the table and held her gaze for a long moment. "It's a little awkward to explain."

"Was it because of Mom?"

Justin sighed. "As I said, she was my best friend's wife.

160

I could never have hurt either of them. Nor could I have offered Allison what she needed and wanted."

"A stable, secure family life?"

He nodded. "I kept in touch for a long time because I couldn't bear not to. When you arrived I kept looking at you and thinking that you could have been my own little girl. I used to send you presents."

"I've kept them, Justin. All of them," Talia told him softly, her eyes growing teary.

He smiled. "I appreciate that. At any rate, one day I just decided I wasn't doing anyone any good trying to maintain what little contact we all had. I knew if I kept returning to your parents' home in between jobs that one day I'd try to leave with Allison. How could I do that to your father? So I just let all contact slip away. It was easier that way."

Talia extended her hand across the table, touching Justin's arm in deep sympathy. "She's alone now, Justin. Do you want her address?"

He looked suddenly stricken. "I couldn't go to her! Not after all these years . . ." So much for the iron-willed assurance of secret agents!

"Why not?"

"I . . . I'll have to think about it," he whispered. "She never knew how I felt."

"It wouldn't be easy going to her, I'll grant you that." Talia grinned with sudden mischief. "You'd have to find her first! She's not the little homebody you once knew. Last I heard she was in Acapulco!"

Justin stared at her in astonishment and then burst out in hearty laughter. "So my little Allison Lee finally decided to see the world!"

"I'm afraid so."

"It might be interesting," he mused, a warm light in his eyes. "There are places I could show her . . ."

The reminiscent talk went on for a long time with Kane becoming actively involved with the conversation as the topic veered from the deeply personal to the more general and highly fascinating one of Justin's former occupation.

By the end of the evening as the three sat sipping cognac in front of the lobby fire, a sprinkling of other inn guests sitting just out of earshot, Talia found herself more and more on the sidelines of the discussion. She didn't mind. She was glad to see Kane as captivated by her mystery man as she was. Perhaps the budding friendship would help soothe the uncertain temper and deep wariness she'd been enduring from her lover all day. Her lover . . . Perhaps she should rephrase that. From the man she loved. She still did not know the depths of his feelings about her. But he wanted her, she told herself as she gazed into the fire. He wanted her and he had proven that, hadn't he? What man would have chased after a woman, offering the only thing he thought he had to attract her, if he didn't want her very badly?

"It's settled, then?" Justin smiled, getting to his feet and glancing absently at the gold watch on his wrist. "I'll see you both down at the dock tomorrow around noon? We can get in a little fishing, Kane, if Talia doesn't mind sitting in the sun and admiring our prowess!" He cocked an eyebrow at her affectionately.

"As long as I don't have to clean them," she agreed cheerfully, rising to stand on tiptoe beside Justin and plant a quick kiss on his cheek. "A boat outing sounds delightful."

"Good." He stood staring down at her for a moment,

shaking his head in disbelief. "Hard to comprehend that after all these years . . ."

"I know," she smiled warmly. "I know."

He took his leave with a crisp handshake for Kane, who folded an arm around Talia's shoulders as they watched him walk out into the night.

"Quite a guy," Kane murmured, guiding her toward the massive staircase that led to the upper level. "Fascinating. Do you realize what a job you did finding him? It's incredible, Talia!"

She laughed, dancing ahead of him into the room as he opened the door. Her eyes were glowing gold as she whirled to face him, the gold zigzag in the black dress catching the light.

"Kane, I could hardly believe it when we found that boat today! It was so exciting! To finally solve the mystery after all these years! When I think of all the government agencies, all the bureaucrats I dealt with! All the clues I followed!"

She looked at him as he walked quietly over to the mirrored dressing table and began loosening his tie. His eyes met hers in the glass and they were very green and enigmatic.

"None of those clues would have gotten me anywhere if you hadn't decided to help me, Kane," she suddenly said. "I owe the final success of all this to you."

"Feeling grateful?" he asked dryly, pulling the tie free and dropping it on the polished chest of drawers.

She blushed, not pretending to misunderstand what he meant. Instead she stepped forward, hands outstretched, her mouth curved into a loving smile.

"Yes," she said as he caught her hands in his own and pulled her toward him.

He didn't return the smile. There was a curious intensity in his eyes as he drew her close, guiding her arms around his neck. Very slowly and deliberately he kissed her, using his expertise to coax her mouth into willing submission. Talia made no attempt to resist. She was in love and the man she loved had just done her a tremendous favor. Yes, she was feeling grateful along with a whole host of other emotions far more powerful than gratitude.

When he lifted his head slowly to gaze down into her dreamy, love-softened eyes, the intensity in him had hardened into something else. He was, she realized vaguely, a man who had come to some inner decision. She stared up at him, wide-eyed and questioning.

"Talia," he growled, his hands working gently on her arms, "Talia, honey, listen to me. Up until now the only thing I've been concentrating on was using whatever it took to push you into an affair. Do you understand? I knew that first day when you walked into my office that I was going to have an affair with you."

"Kane, please, you don't have to talk about this now . . ."

He ignored her small interruption, dismissing it with a quick, negative movement of his head. "I was also determined that you learn right from the beginning that you couldn't manipulate me with little stunts like that damn attempt at blackmail!"

Talia flushed, remembering, but before she could say anything, he was continuing, his voice gritty and tense.

"But I underestimated you. I figured that once I had proven I wasn't about to be intimidated by someone as soft

164

and sweet as you, we could settle down to an affair that would be conducted on my terms. I really thought I had you eating out of the palm of my hand that night after we made love at my place." He grimaced wryly. "I was shocked when you insisted on going back to the hotel, but I told myself you'd calm down by morning. It never occurred to me that you'd leave town! Talk about male ego! And talk about misjudging the power dynamics of a situation!" he added with a rueful twist of his mouth.

"Please," she groaned. "Don't quote my own lectures back at me!"

"But I've learned so much from them," he countered with a flash of humor that quickly disappeared as he went on. "At any rate, I came after you with the only thing I figured I had left to offer. It was obvious you weren't going to come tamely back to Sacramento on command!"

"Kane," Talia whispered, "what are you trying to say?"

"Give me a minute and I'll try and make myself clear." He sighed. "I came after you with the knowledge that I couldn't force you into an affair. My brilliant lovemaking hadn't been enough to convince you, and I had no other choice except to try bargaining. I brought you the information you wanted and offered you a deal. Last night—" He broke off, drawing a deep breath. "Last night when you accepted the bargain and made the first payment on your half of the deal . . ."

Talia winced at the businesslike way he described her love, but she said nothing.

". . . I realized I wasn't getting everything I wanted," he concluded bluntly. "And I'm too damn greedy to settle for less!"

"But, Kane!" Talia looked up at him with suddenly anguished eyes. "What more do you want?"

"I want a hell of a lot more than your gratitude, to begin with," he told her with deep urgency. "I want *more* than your agreement to a business arrangement! And I can wait until you're ready to give me what I want. God knows I've waited long enough for you to walk into my life! But I can't do my waiting while sleeping in the same bed with you! My self-control has some limits."

He released her as if her skin had suddenly become hot beneath his fingers and he stalked over to the dresser. Quickly he pulled out his few clothes and stuffed them into the little leather overnight bag.

"Where are you going, Kane?" Helplessly Talia watched him, trying to make sense out of his actions. "You don't . . . don't want me?"

He shot her a glittering green glance and then went back to his packing. "I want you. I want you so much it's tearing me apart to walk out of here tonight. I'm going to lie awake in another room, which I'm sure the good Mrs. Stanton will be only too happy to give me, and think about what a fool I am for sleeping alone!"

She turned on her heel as he walked past her to the door. "What about the affair you wanted? Kane, I don't understand!"

He paused, his hand on the doorknob, and looked back at her with such need that for a moment she was certain he would come back.

"We're going to have the affair," he promised with such determination she believed him. "But it's going to start off right this time. The next time you lie in my arms it won't be because you're paying off a bargain or because you're feeling grateful!"

He was out the door and on the stairs before Talia recovered her mobility. She stared in stunned amazement at the closed door, listening to his rapidly descending footsteps, and then she launched herself forward.

She wrenched open the door and raced to the edge of the landing, leaning over. He was already on the flight below her.

"Kane!"

He glanced up.

"Kane Sebastian, don't you dare walk out on me!" she cried, heedless of inn guests listening. "If you walk out on me tonight I'll . . . I'll sue you for breach of promise! I'll tell the Sacramento papers how you tried to force me into being your mistress! I'll make sure all your business associates and friends know you stoop to making deals with women! I'll . . . I'll . . ."

Desperately she cast about in her head for further threats as several interested guests began assembling below in the lobby to stare upward. Kane was staring too, as if dazzled by the vision on the floor above.

"More threats, Talia?" he murmured, one hand on the railing. "Are you going to blackmail me into coming back upstairs?

"Yes!"

"Why?" he demanded starkly.

"Because . . . because what I feel isn't gratitude, damn it! Now stop trying to play the martyred, self-denying male tonight! It really doesn't suit you!"

A slow, wickedly affectionate grin relaxed his face. He moved, starting up the stairs with a pacing, pantherish stride that sent a shiver of anticipation down Talia's spine.

"It's not really one of my better roles," he agreed apologetically as he climbed, emerald eyes gleaming. There was a buzz of amused conversation which both of

167

them ignored. "Tell me," Kane went on interestedly, "are all those threats for real?"

"Are you going to call my bluff and find out?" she whispered, clutching the rail for support as she waited for him.

"No," he admitted, reaching the top of the stairs and coming toward her deliberately. "No, I know when I'm beaten. I wouldn't have the nerve to try facing down a practiced little blackmailer like you. Quite ruthless, aren't you?"

He reached her, taking hold of her arm and propelling her lightly back into the room. He shut the door with a finality that must have satisfied the curious onlookers at the bottom of the stairs.

He set down the leather bag and hauled her tightly against him.

"Talia," he growled, suddenly very serious. "Talia, my sweet, do you want me so much?"

"Yes." It was the simple truth. She clung to him, face buried against his shirt. In time, she swore to herself, in time she would tell him the whole truth. The truth about her love for him. But for tonight she would be satisfied.

"It's not just gratitude?" he pressed her, his fingers stroking the length of her spine in caressing movements that arched her closely into him.

"It never was. Oh, Kane, I . . . I started wanting you that first day!"

She felt him tremble at the softly voiced confession and the hands stroking her back became warmer, more enticing.

"Thank you, Talia," he murmured into her hair. "Thank you for giving me that much. By this afternoon

I realized I couldn't bear the thought of forcing you to stay with me out of gratitude or because of our arrangement. I knew that I could make you admit you wanted me when I took you in my arms, but it wasn't the same as hearing you say it outside of bed. In the throes of passion people will say a great deal. But I want more than a bedroom relationship with you. A lot more. Talia, I love you!"

If he hadn't been holding her so tightly, Talia was certain she would have collapsed.

"Oh, Kane! Is that the truth? I think I've loved you from the beginning."

"Darling," he whispered, eyes raking her with green fire. "Are you certain? It's not just gratitude or . . . or . . ."

"Gratitude it is not!" she declared passionately. "In fact, there are a few things, Kane Sebastian, for which I may never forgive you! It has to be love. There's no other explanation for my behavior! Imagine falling in love with a man who wouldn't even submit gracefully to a little honest blackmail!"

"When I found myself chasing after you, begging to pay the ransom, I realized I was feeling a hell of a lot more than mere attraction." He grinned in delight. "Do you think I usually allow a woman to manipulate me so easily?"

"I haven't manipulated you! You made it very clear from the beginning that everything would be on your terms!"

"And I failed every time I tried to enforce my terms! You've now intimidated me to the point where I publicly succumb to threats and meekly follow orders! What do you suppose the other guests must think of me?" He laughed huskily, his fingers moving on her black dress.

169

"There I was, climbing those stairs on command like a lamb to the slaughter."

"What an awful thing to say!"

"Have pity on your victim, darling, he's been through a lot."

The black dress slid into a pool at her feet as Kane opened the fastening. It was followed a moment later by the shirt he had been wearing.

Moments later they stood naked together and Kane stepped back, his eyes scorching Talia's gleaming body. "You're so lovely, so soft and warm and inviting. Do you know what it does to me to know how you respond to my touch?" He moved his hand to cup her breast, gently caressing the nipple until it firmed. Talia trembled and threw her arms around his neck.

"An ego trip?" she guessed, smiling a teasing smile. "Does it give you a pleasant feeling of power to know what you do to me?"

"It's a two-edged sword," he replied, the hard planes of his face tautening with the leaping urgency of passion. "On the one hand it makes me feel as if I were at the head of a conquering army." He stooped, lifting her into his arms and carrying her toward the bed. "But on the other hand it makes me realize how vulnerable I am. I can't stand the thought of your tiring of me, of no longer responding to me. Or, even worse, of your finding someone else. I told you, I'm a greedy man. I want sole claim on your passion! God, I love you, sweetheart!"

He settled her under the old-fashioned quilt, standing for a moment beside the bed to gaze down at her. A fan of tawny hair framed her face as she lay waiting for him with eyes of heated gold.

"Ask me," he urged softly. "Ask me to make love to you. I want to know you need me!"

How could she deny him?

"Please come to bed and make love to me, my darling Kane. Let me show you how much I love you." She held open her arms, her love shining in her eyes.

"Talia! I'll give you anything you want," he rasped, coming to her with a flaming desire that intoxicated her. "Anything. Just go on loving me forever!"

He gathered her to him, deep hungry kisses parting her lips as his hands began gliding possessively over her body.

"You're all I want," she managed to whisper and the instant response in him was glorious to know.

She opened up her senses to the full impact of him and was content. There had been no talk of marriage, but all her instincts were serene. Kane loved her. Whether or not he ever offered marriage, she knew she would always be able to trust his love. And wasn't that the most important thing? Perhaps, in time, he would want the more formal commitment, but for now she would be satisfied.

"Talia, my lady of silk and fire," he said huskily against the curve of her breast. His touch floated over her, at times tantalizing and teasing, at times excitingly raspy and demanding. She arched into every caress, twisted with delight into every new invitation.

Her fingertips danced along his spine, down to the muscular buttocks, and sank deeply into the hard male flesh. His body surged against hers and his deeply muttered groan set off waves of delight in her.

"Oh, Kane! My darling Kane!"

She heard his sharply drawn breath as he found her softening, damp warmth. She rose higher and higher to the peak of sensual excitement, as tiny, stifled sounds

171

escaped from the back of her throat. They seemed to inflame Kane in turn.

"Talk to me," he pleaded savagely. "Talk to me of love. Tell me how much you need me . . ."

"I think you must know everything there is to know about that subject," she managed breathlessly, her fingers twisting in his hair. "You turn me into a creature I didn't know existed!"

"I knew she existed," he grated, his tongue darting out to curl into the pit of her stomach as he tenderly clenched her thighs. "I knew she existed the day you walked into my office and dared to threaten me! I had to make certain it was *me* that delicious creature needed. I had to bind you to me, Talia. That's why I strung out that lie to keep you in Sacramento. I needed time."

She moaned as he used his teeth very lovingly on the insides of her thighs. Her senses raced in mad, swirling circles.

The magic became tighter and stronger as Kane lavished the full extent of his potent masculine arsenal on her. In turn Talia gloried in his response to her, telling him of her love in the countless ways a woman discovers when she's finally and completely in love.

The golden time in the huge four-poster bed went by unmeasured. Kane warmed Talia's body until she thought she would literally go up in flames. His lips sought out every inch of her and made it his own. The fierce, drowning kisses swamped her as they nipped at her earlobe, laved the curve of her shoulder, flicked the tips of her breasts, and explored the contour of her waist.

Over and over again he repeated the sensuous, mind-spinning kisses and all the while his sensitive fingers traced

172

unimaginable patterns of desire across the small mound below her waist and into the secret core of her femininity.

"Please, Kane! I don't think I can take anymore. Come to me, now!"

"I don't think I could wait any longer if I tried," he confessed almost violently as he rose above her, seeking a place between her legs. "Make me a part of you, my lovely Talia. I need you so much!"

She clung to him, pulling him to her with all the strength at her command and he mastered her body in a hot rush of need that sent shock waves through her.

The waves never had time to settle. Instantly they were reinforced by the erotic rhythm Kane established. Each powerful movement of his body on hers fed the delicious energy that enveloped them, sending it to staggering levels that threatened to consume them both.

And eventually it did. Talia's cry of wonder was answered by Kane's hoarse, muffled shout. There was conquest and victory and surrender and supplication involved, but it would have been impossible to sort out the emotions and assign them to either party. They were all wrapped up together, an integral part of the magic. The vulnerability went hand-in-hand with the raging desire.

A two-edged sword.

CHAPTER TEN

A truly contented and satisfied male was a magnificent and amusing creature, Talia decided the next morning as she carefully chose a bag of preservative-free potato chips and dropped it into her shopping cart.

Her mouth quirked in silent humor as she thought of Kane's buoyant and thoroughly charming mood that morning as he'd left for the docks, cameras slung across each shoulder. He had awakened practically purring. It reminded her of a dragon's purr, she decided as she chose some imported beer.

But, then, she must have been in a pretty good mood herself, to agree to do the shopping for the boat outing Justin had promised. Here she was, traipsing up and down grocery aisles, while the men lounged around the boat and counted bait. Kane had been eager for some picturesque harbor shots which she knew she would be privileged to view at a later date. Photographers! Ah, well. There were worse hobbies.

It struck her as she moved toward the checkout counter that she was going to have to find another hobby herself. Justin Gage Westbrook was a solved puzzle. If she weren't careful, Kane would talk her into learning photography and she would wind up going everywhere draped with cameras and equipment!

She was still thinking of the previous night and of the warmth in Kane's eyes that morning when she drove the Lotus down to the harbor and parked it. She had made him happy and the knowledge gave her a sense of well being unlike anything she'd ever known. Of course, she reflected as she reached for the sacks of groceries, it worked both ways! Her own happiness had put a glow in her eyes that even she herself could detect. Her body felt wonderful, caressed and loved.

She glanced automatically toward Justin's boat in the distance and nearly dropped both bags at the sight of the figure ahead of her.

Aaron Pomeroy!

For a moment she couldn't move. Her only thought was the useless one of trying to shout a warning. It would never be heard. Guilt welled up. She'd led Pomeroy here, given him the clues that had eventually led to Justin!

Kane was on that boat! It was what finally galvanized her into motion. She had to do something, and quickly.

Hurrying forward, she reached into one of her sacks and lifted out a six-pack of beer. Waving it merrily at the occupants of the nearest boat, she yelled cheerfully,

"Hey, there's a party down at the *Allison Lee*. Come on!"

No one needed a second invitation. With welcoming, laughing shouts, people who had been idling or working

175

on their boats leaped to the docks to follow. Each called to others en route until Talia was surrounded by an eager, jesting crowd.

"Hey! I saw you yesterday, honey. I suppose that guy who had his arm around you owns you?"

Talia was saved a direct answer as another voice broke in to ask if more beer would be needed.

"I've got a couple of six-packs."

"Here's the ice!"

Talia thought she saw Pomeroy ahead of her edging onto the *Allison Lee*. She hurried, urging the flock of good-natured people around her to quicken their pace. They did so gladly, several pushing to board the boat.

They all reached the *Allison Lee* in a shouting, laughing chunk of humanity that washed onto the blue and white boat en masse.

What happened next happened quickly.

Talia was on the edge of the dock, about to board with several others, when Aaron Pomeroy realized his dilemma. He had just stepped on himself and was nearly swallowed up in the rush of eager party-goers. Hastily he backed away, his hand diving under the edge of his jacket.

At that moment Justin emerged from the cabin, staring in astonishment at the people surging on board.

Desperately Talia waved at him, trying to point out Pomeroy. At that instant Pomeroy turned, catching sight of Talia. Rage replaced the panic that had begun to grow in the marble eyes. He shoved at the nearest innocent bystander, pushing him out of the way, and bounded toward the edge of the dock. A wicked-looking gun had appeared in one hand.

Talia barely had time to assess the anger and fear in the

cold brown eyes before a furious shout sounded behind her.

"Talia! Jump!"

It was Kane's voice. She didn't hesitate. Without even thinking about it, Talia leaped off the edge of the small gangplank she had started to cross. She landed in the water with a resounding splash, the groceries cascading around her into the depths. A shot crackled in the air where she had stood.

Her first thought as the dark green water covered her head was to close her eyes in order to keep the contact lenses from being washed away. It was an instinctive habit wearers of contact lenses developed early and it somehow seemed more important than worrying about nearly being shot by Aaron Pomeroy.

That was most important until she remembered that Kane's voice had been coming from behind her! He would have been the next in line as a target for Pomeroy.

Desperately Talia struck out for the surface. Exploding above it in a rush, she flipped her hair hastily back from her eyes and opened them to see Kane leaning over the edge of the dock. Aaron Pomeroy lay very still at his feet, several fishermen hovering around him with a variety of ropes.

She thought she detected concern in the green eyes, but the moment Kane saw she was all right the light of pure deviltry replaced the first emotion. He unslung the camera from around his neck.

"Hold it right there. This is going to be a memorable shot!"

"You idiot! What happened to Pomeroy!"

"I hit him, naturally. He was so busy trying to shoot

177

you he didn't see me until it was too late. Now smile!" He began focusing the camera.

"You two make a great team," Justin announced, leaning over the edge of the *Allison Lee*'s railing. "Talia creates the action and Kane immortalizes it on film. Practice a lot together?"

"I had no idea she was going to be such a natural model. Really knows how to liven up a shot, doesn't she? Stop glaring at me, honey. New brides are supposed to be happy creatures!"

"Kane Sebastian, I've warned you before about telling social lies," Talia yelled up at him, but her heart was singing.

"A nasty habit of mine which you can cure very easily, my love." He grinned, hurriedly snapping pictures of Talia as she swam for the dock. Several willing hands were already reaching down to assist her.

"Are you suggesting I make an honest man out of you?" she grumbled as she was hauled, dripping, up onto the dock. She turned to face him, swiping at the water in her clothes in useless gestures. A delighted crowd waited expectantly for Kane's answer.

"Think of the embarrassment it would save in the future!" He lifted his camera once again for a final shot.

"If you're asking me to marry you, you can damn well come out from behind that camera and do it properly!"

"Maybe I should use some of these shots to blackmail you into marrying me. Think what your management seminar students would say if they saw their instructor in this condition. Very bad for the public image, you know . . ."

"Kane!"

He dropped the camera to his side, stepping heedlessly

over Pomeroy's body to take her into his arms. "Of course I'm asking you to marry me, you little nitwit," he murmured lovingly. "I knew I was going to marry you that night I first announced our engagement to Fairfax."

Above the laughter and good-natured comments of the crowd, Talia whispered wonderingly, "The night you told Richard you were going to marry me? You knew it then?"

"Darling, no wonder you have a little trouble wielding things like power and blackmail. You don't seem to know when your victim is truly under control."

She smiled up at him very brilliantly. "Are you really under my control, Kane?"

"Since the day you walked into my office," he assured her, not looking overly concerned by the fact. "Are you going to give me my answer so all these nice people will witness a happy ending?"

Her smile broadened into a teasing grin as she wrapped her arms around his neck and pressed her wet body close to him. "And if I don't? If I decide to string you along a little?"

"Then I shall toss you back into the harbor and keep you there until you see fit to come around to my way of thinking," he promised imperturbably.

"As I've often said," she sighed blissfully, "you don't need any lessons in management technique. You're a natural. I accept."

He kissed her very thoroughly as Justin Westbrook and the surrounding crowd cheered.

Much later that afternoon Talia stretched out her legs, clad now in another new pair of jeans, and reached up to accept the icy beer Kane was handing her. The *Allison Lee* still bobbed quietly alongside the dock, the fishing trip postponed until the following day. Justin had had his hands full for the past few hours arranging to have Aaron Pomeroy discreetly picked up by a couple of very business-like members of the real FBI. The Bureau, it seemed, owed a favor or two to the Department. It was willing to take Pomeroy off Justin's hands until McCary could get out to the West Coast. The Bureau was also not particularly impressed with Pomeroy's false identification. The crowd from the surrounding boats had been fed a reasonable tale of attempted robbery foiled by the timely arrival of Talia. Nobody pressed for more information than was volunteered. Small-town fishing people had a deeply ingrained sense of respect for the privacy of others.

"You sure go through clothes, woman," Kane complained cheerfully as he dropped into the seat beside her and reached for the bowl of potato chips Justin had been monopolizing. "You're going to have to cut back after we're married. I refuse to spring for a new pair of jeans every day!"

Talia pursed her lips sulkily. "Setting down rules and regulations already?"

"It's called drawing in the rein, and make no mistake about it, I'm going to keep you on a very short one. No more stunts like that rescue attempt today, understood? I swear to God! The sight of Pomeroy aiming that gun at you must have aged me by about ten years!"

"Actually," Justin interposed thoughtfully, "all things considered, it was a rather clever move. I do believe you inherited your father's talent for thinking on his feet. Cameron was pretty good at that, you know. I told you last night you had good instincts. Today you proved you can act in a hurry—"

"Justin," Kane interrupted, eyeing the other man

180

through narrowed lids. "If you're about to suggest what I think you are . . ."

"What is it, Justin?" Talia demanded, glowing beneath the praise. She shot a meaningful glance at Kane, willing him to shut up.

"Well, my dear, you did say you weren't overly fond of your present job . . ."

"No!" Kane exploded, sitting up abruptly.

"I'm beginning to get the feeling this isn't going to be a popular suggestion," Justin murmured apologetically.

"I want to hear it. Be quiet, Kane!"

"I was only going to say that the one thing the Intelligence business can always use more of is . . . intelligence. Too many of the Pomeroy types around. It's a miracle the man even managed to follow you two here . . ." He broke off as Kane started to interrupt once more. "Simmer down, Kane. I was only going to suggest a nice, safe desk job. McCary would be interested, I'm sure, and since Talia doesn't care for her present job . . ."

"Forget it!" Kane growled, refusing to pay any attention to Talia's interested expression. "I consider myself a reasonably liberated male."

"Hah!" Talia's pithy interruption didn't phase Kane.

"But I'll be damned if my wife is going to work as some sort of secret agent! She has a perfectly good career as it is and she's more than ready for the next step in it!" he declared.

"I am?" Talia looked at him blankly.

"Definitely," he confirmed with a brisk nod. "It's obvious the time has come for you to open up your own school of management. Perhaps your boss would be interested in selling you an Advanced Management Designs franchise.

Sacramento could use something like that," he added deliberately.

"It could?" Talia looked at him, much struck by the idea.

"Naturally. And if it isn't, you can see to it that it gets ready. You've got everything you need to make it successfully on your own, sweetheart. You're smart, you're persistent, and you've got all the basic skills. As your own boss you won't have the problem of competing in a corporate structure and there's a lot more satisfaction in being the head of an operation rather than a vice-president. Ask me, I know."

"Oh, Kane . . ." Talia was entranced. She had never thought of trying something totally on her own. Her education, her thinking, and her background had all been aimed at surviving in large corporations. Why hadn't it occurred to her to try the independent route?

"I don't know where you were at in terms of confidence three years ago, but believe me, you're not short of it now! You didn't think twice about flattening Richard Fairfax at that restaurant that night. You were quite willing to try a little blackmail on me and you moved in on Pomeroy this afternoon as if you'd planned the whole operation in advance. Furthermore, you had the confidence to trust your own instincts when the chips were down. You distrusted Pomeroy, believed in Justin, and trusted me. You've obviously developed into a fairly good judge of human nature in the past three years and that's a very useful quality in the business world. You can do it, honey," he concluded earnestly, green eyes very certain and full of confidence in her. "You can set up your own business and get to the top all on your own!"

A slow smile curved Talia's lips as she got thoughtfully

to her feet and strolled over to dig out another can of beer. *All on her own.* It was a nice thought. She could be the president of her own company and she could sell the one thing she really did well—management training skills. It was a perfect answer.

Not finding any beer left in the ice chest, she wandered into the cabin and searched the galley, her mind spinning with thoughts and plans. A few minutes later she emerged silently, can in hand, in time to hear the end of a comment Justin was making to Kane in a soft, amused tone of voice.

". . . have to hand it to you, that wasn't a bad move on your part. Very neatly solves the problem of getting her to Sacramento, for one thing. And I think she'll make it. After all, she *is* Cameron's daughter."

"Not to mention the fact," Kane finished smoothly, "that if anyone dares get in her way this time, I'll slaughter him." He took a contented sip of his beer.

Talia moved forward, her free hand resting aggressively on her hip. "For that chauvinistic, overly protective male remark, Kane Sebastian, you can buy dinner tonight."

"But I bought it last night," he protested, looking up at her with gleaming eyes.

"Tough."

"You see?" Kane said to Justin in an aggrieved tone. "She runs roughshod over me."

Justin laughed. "In honor of the wedding I'm going to be attending shortly, *I* will pay for dinner tonight!"

Talia smiled at him as Kane caught her hand in his and tugged her closer. "And then what will you do, Justin?"

"After the wedding? Why, I think I'll take a little trip down to Acapulco to see if I can intercept that cruise ship your mother is on . . ."

"You still have a passport?" Kane asked interestedly.

"Several," Justin said dryly. "One of the fringe benefits of the trade."

Four days later Talia's eyes flickered open lazily as she came awake in the warm, protective arms of her new husband. For a moment she lay still, savoring the happiness that was hers and then she could stand it no longer. She had to stretch.

"Ouch!" Kane moved his knee out of the way. "You do tend to wriggle in the mornings, don't you, honey?" He yawned magnificently into the soft tangle of her hair and hugged her a little closer.

Talia wriggled again, delightfully, when his palm came into delicious contact with the tip of her breast. Kane murmured something unintelligible against the nape of her neck.

"What did you say?"

"I said it's a good thing I don't play golf. A serious golfer would be out there on the fairways this morning instead of lying in bed with his new bride." He nodded briefly in the direction of the golf course that lay beyond the huge bedroom window.

"Whereas a serious photographer . . . ?"

"Whereas a serious *husband and lover*," he corrected easily, "is content to indulge in indoor hobbies." The warm hand on her breast tightened and the lazy humor in him disappeared to be replaced by the beginnings of passion. "I love you, Talia."

She turned toward him, her fingers trailing through the red curls of his chest hair. Her golden eyes glowed. "And I love you. More than I can ever say, Kane."

"Then you can show me, instead," he drawled, eyes darkening into green fires. His hand slipped down the silky length of her side to rest invitingly on her hip. "And go on showing me for the rest of our lives."

"On the theory that one picture is worth a thousand words?" Already her body was coming alive beneath his touch. She responded to the growing heat in him with a willing passion.

"Something like that. We might make a photographer out of you yet. Looking forward to your new career, Mrs. Sebastian?"

"You mean as president of Sacramento's newest center for management training?" she murmured, shivering as Kane's caresses grew more deliberately sensual.

"I was referring to your other important career." He brushed his lips tantalizingly along the line of her throat as Talia's fingers sank luxuriously into the skin of his shoulder.

"Ah, you mean that of managing Kane Sebastian? Why, yes, I am. I intend to stand at the top of my profession."

"Want a few hints?"

"Certainly. I'm always ready to learn."

"To begin with, success in your new field isn't necessarily obtained in a standing position."

"No?"

"No. Your present position, in fact, will be far more conducive to total management control."

"I'm listening."

"It's also a good policy to give the poor soul being managed a nice sense of security," he went on knowledgeably.

"And how would you suggest I do that?"

"By telling him over and over again how much you love him."

"Fortunately," Talia whispered huskily, "I have a real talent for that. I love you, Kane."

He gathered her into his arms with undisguised need and love. A need and a love, Talia's instincts told her, that would last a lifetime.

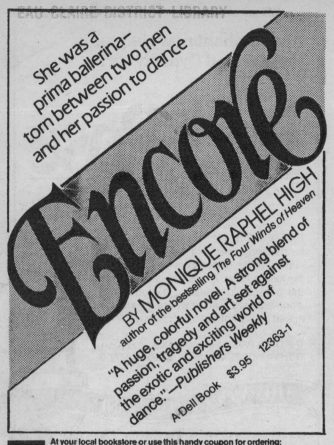